Critical Acclaim For
Ross Thomas
(and Oliver Bleeck)
and
THE BRASS GO-BETWEEN

•

"The best political-suspense-story writer going."
— *Houston Post*

•

'Bleeck writes like Ross Macdonald with a sense of humor."
— *Miami Herald*

•

"A wild caper."
— *Library Journal*

•

"The work of an accomplished writer....Highly recommended."
— *Publishers Weekly*

•

more ...

"The best of the American practitioners of the skulk and dagger genre ... anyone reading a Ross Thomas thriller for the first time is in imminent danger of addiction."
— *Los Angeles Times*

●

"This is fiction with a flair.... The author has a sharp, polished style and his hero is full of dry wit, intelligence, and savoir-faire."
— *Associated Press*

●

"Our hero is pleasing, his adventures exciting, his African contacts, for better of worse, delightful, and his heart is finally in the right place."
— *Times Literary Supplement*

●

"Ross Thomas is that rare phenomenon, a writer of suspense novels whose books can be read with pleasure more than once."
— **Eric Ambler**

●

"Rates with the highest marks in his particular field."
— **Margaret Manning,** *Boston Globe*

●

"Thomas is one of our leading beguilers."
— *Philadelphia Inquirer*

●

Also by Ross Thomas

VOODOO, LTD.
TWILIGHT AT MAC'S PLACE
THE FOURTH DURANGO
OUT ON THE RIM
BRIARPATCH
MISSIONARY STEW
THE MORDIDA MAN
THE EIGHTH DWARF
CHINAMAN'S CHANCE
YELLOW-DOG CONTRACT
THE MONEY HARVEST
IF YOU CAN'T BE GOOD
THE PORKCHOPPERS
THE BACKUP MEN
THE FOOLS IN TOWN ARE ON OUR SIDE
THE SINGAPORE WINK
CAST A YELLOW SHADOW
THE COLD WAR SWAP

Under the Pseudonym Oliver Bleeck

NO QUESTIONS ASKED
THE HIGHBINDERS
THE PROCANE CHRONICLE
PROTOCOL FOR A KIDNAPPING
THE BRASS GO-BETWEEN

ROSS THOMAS

WRITING AS OLIVER BLEECK

THE BRASS GO-BETWEEN

THE MYSTERIOUS PRESS

Published by Warner Books

A Time Warner Company

MYSTERIOUS PRESS EDITION

Cover Design & Illustration by Peter Thorpe

The Mysterious Press Edition is published by arrangement with the author.

The Mysterious Press name and logo are trademarks of Warner Books, Inc.

 Mysterious Press Books are published by
Warner Books, Inc.
1271 Avenue of the Americas
New York, NY 10020

 A Time Warner Company

Printed in the United States of America

First Mysterious Press Printing: June 1993
10 9 8 7 6 5 4 3 2 1

1

The choice was simple enough. I could either answer the knock at the door or draw to a three-card diamond flush, a foolhardy act usually associated with those who maintain an abiding faith in elves, political platforms, and money-back guarantees. The door and whoever was behind it, even the Avon lady, seemed by far the more promising, so I threw in my hand, opened the door, and was only slightly disappointed when the knocker turned out to be Myron Greene, the lawyer, who announced, a little too loudly, I thought, that he needed to speak to me in private.

The game was at my place that Saturday, five-card stud and draw, and it was to go on all day and into the night. There were five of us and we had started at ten-thirty in the morning and by midafternoon when Myron Greene, the lawyer, knocked at the door, I was almost six hundred dollars ahead. I was living on the ninth floor of the Adelphi on East 46th and the only private place was the bathroom so we went in there. I closed the door, sat on the edge of the tub, and let Myron Greene have the one thing that resembled a chair. He lowered the lid and sat down, crossed his plump legs, took off his glasses, polished them with a silk tie that was fashionably wide, and breathed as he always did, a little asthmatically.

"You're not answering your mail," he said.

"I'm not even reading it."

"You're not answering your phone either."

"The desk is taking messages. I pick them up once a day."

"I left four messages yesterday. Urgent ones."

"I forgot to check yesterday."

"I had to drive all the way in from Darien," Myron Greene said, and there was reproof and even petulance in his voice.

"Couldn't it have waited till Monday?" I said. "I start answering the phone again on Monday."

"No," Myron Greene said, "it couldn't wait. You have to be there on Monday."

I could never bring myself to refer to Myron Greene as *my* lawyer and that wasn't because I didn't like him or his fees weren't high enough. It was just that Myron Greene didn't fit a carefully preconceived notion of what *my* lawyer should be. This notion had my lawyer as a seedy, garrulous old goat with rheumy eyes, a rusty alpaca suit on his back, a string tie at his throat and larceny in his heart who operated out of a dingy walk-up office that he shared with a bail bondsman down near City Hall. Tufts of gray hair also grew out of his ears.

By contrast Myron Greene was a sleek, overweight thirty-five who dressed several daring (for him) sartorial degrees to the left of Brooks Brothers, had offices on Madison, a home in Darien, and clients, but for me, with six- and seven-figure bank accounts or Inc. behind their names and branch offices in Houston and Los Angeles. I was always vaguely disappointed when I talked to Myron Greene. I kept hoping to find a spot of gravy on a lapel or an unnoticed blob of mayonnaise on a tie, but I never did, and consequently Myron Greene remained *the* lawyer.

"Where do I have to be Monday?" I said.

"Washington."

"Why?"

"A shield," Myron Greene said. "It's missing."

"From where?"

"A museum. The Coulter."

"Why me?"

"They asked for you."

"The museum?"

"No," Myron Greene said. "The other side. The thieves."

"How much?"

"A quarter of a million."

"What is it, gold?"

"No. It's brass."

"Usual terms?"

He nodded. "Ten percent."

"Do I need it?"

Myron Greene crossed his legs the other way, fingered one slightly peaked lapel of his eight-button, double-breasted cavalry twill jacket, and smiled at me with white, remarkably even teeth that had had a dentist's careful attention four times a year for the past thirty-two years. "Your wife," he said.

"My ex-wife."

"Her lawyer called."

"And?"

"Your son starts to school next month. The call was to remind me that your support payments go up two hundred a month."

"Well, two hundred a month should pay for his eleven o'clock milk and cookies. I wouldn't want him to have to brown-bag it."

3

"It's a special school," Myron Greene said.

"The fancy private one that she was always talking about?"

"That's it."

"What's wrong with a public kindergarten?" I said.

Myron Greene smiled again. "Your son's 164 IQ and your ex-wife."

"Mostly my ex-wife."

"Mostly."

"I heard she was getting married."

"Not for a while," he said. "Not until May. When school's out."

"If the payments go up two hundred a month, that'll make it an even thousand—right?"

"Right."

"Then I need the money."

Myron Greene nodded and carefully smoothed a hand over his brown hair that just escaped being too long—too long for an uptown lawyer anyway. The length of his hair was like the clothes he wore and the Excalibur he drove. They served to hint, but only hint, at what he knew the real Myron Greene to be— the one who, were it not for the house in Darien, the cottage in Kennebunkport, the wife (his first), the three kids (two boys and a girl), the firm, and the clients—especially the clients—would be out there where it's really at, his mind and imagination unfettered, his sex life rich and varied, and his soul his own and in perfect step with the sound of that different drummer. That's the real reason why I was Myron Greene's client: he mistakenly thought that I knew the drummer by his first name.

"Tell me some more about the shield," I said.

Myron Greene reached into the inside pocket of his jacket and brought out an envelope. "I dictated it yesterday after I couldn't reach you," he said, and tapped the envelope against the yellow American Standard lavatory. "I didn't know if you would be here. If you weren't, I was going to slip it under the door."

4

"You want to tell me about it now that I'm here?"

He looked at his watch, a gold chronometer which I was sure could tell him what time it was in Shanghai. "I don't have much time now."

"Neither do I."

Myron Greene sniffed at that. Anyone who played cards in the middle of the afternoon had all the time there was.

"Briefly," I said.

"All right," he said. "Briefly. But it's all in here." He quit tapping the envelope against the lavatory and handed it to me.

"I'll read it when the game breaks up."

"If you can spare the time." Myron Greene wasn't very good at sarcasm.

"Briefly," I said again.

"All right. Three days ago—that would be Thursday, wouldn't it?"

"Thursday."

"On Thursday the Coulter Museum in Washington opened a two-month-long exhibition of African art. It's been on tour for almost a year—Rome, Frankfurt, Paris, London, and Moscow. Washington's the final exhibition. The same night that it opened, Thursday night, the prize piece was stolen. Just one piece. It's a brass shield about a yard in diameter and about seven or eight hundred years old. Or older. Anyway it's invaluable and whoever stole it wants $250,000 to return it and they want you to handle the negotiations. That's why the museum people got in touch with me; that's why I tried to reach you. The museum is agreeable to the price." Myron Greene stood up and glanced at his watch again. "Now I *am* late." He made a vague gesture toward the envelope that I held. "It's all in there."

"Okay," I said. "I'll read it after the game."

"Are you ahead?" he asked, and I knew he wanted me to say no.

"Yes."

5

"How much?" It's not something you ask, but Myron Greene did. If I were ahead enough, it might be even better.

"I don't know," I said. "About six hundred."

"That much?"

"That much. Would you like to sit in?"

Myron Greene moved toward the bathroom door, toward the wife and the kids and the firm and the Chris-Craft up in Maine. "No, I guess not. Not this time anyway. I'm really awfully late. Is it a regular game?"

"More or less," I said. "There are about fifteen of us, but usually only five or six can make it at any one time. They drift in and out. Come on, I'll introduce you."

"Well, I don't think—"

"Come on."

He met them all. He met Henry Knight, who had the lead in a play that had managed to run for fourteen weeks despite the critics' indifference, if not their hostility. Knight, cast in yet another juvenile lead at forty-two, agreed with the critics and considered each pay check to be pure lagniappe. He spent his money as quickly as he got it and poker was not only fast, but pleasant, and didn't necessarily entail a hangover. Knight was down almost two hundred dollars and when Myron Greene told him that he liked his current play, Knight said, "It took a lot of wonderful people to create such a wonderful piece of shit."

Myron Greene met Johnny Parisi, recently paroled from Sing-Sing, where he had been doing a three-to-seven on an involuntary manslaughter conviction. Parisi ran with the Ducci brothers over in Brooklyn doing, as he had once testified in court, "this and that." Parisi had played basketball for some small college in Pennsylvania and even made it through his junior year before they caught him shaving points. He was now in his mid-thirties, almost six-foot-five, still lean, and somehow vaguely handsome. He kept a

6

long amber cigarette holder clenched between his teeth even when he wasn't smoking and talked through or around it. I had to keep asking him what he said. He was into the game for about four hundred and most of it was piled in front of the man on his left who, by rights, should have arrested Parisi for parole violation. The man was Lieutenant Kenneth Ogden of the vice squad, sometimes known as Ogden the Odd, and nobody ever asked him where he got the money to play table-stakes poker, although a couple of his cronies claimed that his wife had money. If she did, she had a lot. Ogden was over fifty, looked older, and dressed better than either Knight or Parisi, both of whom were regarded as dudes in their respective social circles. Parisi mumbled something around his cigarette holder when I introduced Myron Greene; Ogden said "hi yah" and kept on shuffling the cards.

The fourth man that Myron Greene met wore chinos, a sweatshirt emblazoned with "Bluebird Inn Keglers," and dirty white sneakers. He was Park Tyler Wisdom III, and he did absolutely nothing for a living because his grandmother had left him a seven-million-dollar trust fund when he was twenty-two. Occasionally, Wisdom would join some protest march or other and once he had been hauled in for burning what he claimed to have been his draft card, but no charges were lodged after the Federal authorities were quietly reminded that Wisdom held the Silver Star and the Purple Heart with a cluster for something he had once done during the two years he had spent with the First Air Cavalry in Vietnam. Now twenty-nine, Wisdom was a little below average height and a little above average weight. To me he looked like nothing more than a rapidly aging Puck for whom the joke got better every year. He said "hello" cheerfully enough to Myron Greene despite the fact that most of my six hundred dollars had come from him.

None of them was interested in the lawyer if he didn't want to sit in, so I walked him to the elevator and when we were in the hall he stopped, turned to me, and said, "Isn't that the Parisi who—"

"The same," I said.

The real Myron Greene stood up. Gone was the dream of the carefree, reckless life. This was Citizen Greene, an officer of the court. "Gambling is a parole violation," Citizen Greene said. "That detective should—"

"Lieutenant," I said. "He's in vice. Besides, he's winning all of Parisi's money."

Myron Greene shook his head as he punched the button for the elevator. "I don't know where you find them."

"They're friends and acquaintances," I said. "If they weren't friends and acquaintances, I wouldn't be of much use to you, would I?"

He seemed to think about my question for a moment and apparently concluded that it didn't deserve an answer. He had his own question. "You'll read that memo I gave you?"

"When the game breaks up."

"They expect you in Washington Monday."

"So you said."

"Call me at home tomorrow and let me know what you decide."

"All right."

"You need the money, you know."

"I know."

Myron Greene shook his head sadly as he waited for the elevator. "A killer and a cop," he said.

"It's the kind of world we live in."

"Your kind maybe; not mine."

"All right."

For Myron Greene the sound of the different drummer had faded. The elevator came and he stepped into it, turned, and stared at me. "The least you could do is answer your phone," he said as we waited there for the doors to close. If I started answering my phone when it rang, I might be on the path to redemption.

"Tomorrow," I said. "I'll answer it tomorrow."

"Today," he insisted. "Something might happen."

I was six hundred ahead so I could afford to lose a little. "Okay," I said. "Today."

The doors began to close and Myron Greene nodded at me brusquely. I took it for a gesture of encouragement, one that would help me to shed my slothful ways, shun my evil companions, and even answer the telephone on its first ring.

2

There must be a few places hotter than Washington in August. The Spice Islands, I suppose. Death Valley. Perhaps Chad down around Bokoro. *The Washington Post* that I read in the non-air-conditioned taxi that bore me from National Airport to the Madison had a small feature on page one boasting about how yesterday had been the hottest August day on record and that today should prove even hotter than that.

Congress had given up for a while and gone home the week before after accomplishing neither more nor less than usual. It wasn't an election year, not that it mattered, and home—wherever it was, even Scottsdale, Arizona—was probably cooler than Washington. The Capital's two major attractions, the Cherry Blossom Festival and the annual riot, had come and gone, the first in April, the second in July. So with Congress adjourned, the lobbyists on vacation, and even the tourists skittish of sunstroke, the lobby of the Madison was virtually deserted except for a couple of bored bellhops who looked as though they were seriously considering another profession.

The clerk at the reservation desk seemed delighted to have something to do when I asked if there was a reservation for Philip St. Ives. There was and I sneezed at the abrupt change in temperature all the way up to the sixth floor, where one of the bellhops fiddled with the air-conditioning controls while making some pertinent comments about the weather.

After he left, the richer by a dollar, I took out the envelope that Myron Greene had given me Saturday and checked a name and a phone number. I dialed the number and when the operator's voice said, "Coulter Museum," I said, "Mrs. Frances Wingo, please." After the operator there was only one secretary to go through. Then the next voice said, "This is Frances Wingo, Mr. St. Ives. I've been expecting your call." It was a good telephone voice for a woman, a shade above contralto with a confident, penetrating quality which convinced me that no one ever called her Frannie.

"Myron Greene mentioned a meeting," I said. "But he didn't mention the time."

"One o'clock. For lunch, if that's convenient."

"It is. Where?"

"Here at the museum. There'll be the two of us and the three-man executive committee. Any cab driver will know where it is."

"At one o'clock then," I said.

"At one," she said.

After we hung up I read through Myron Greene's three-page memorandum again, but there was nothing in it that I had missed from previous readings. I had little else to do for the next 45 minutes so I took out my wallet and counted the money. There was a trifle more than $400. I had emerged at 3 A.M. Sunday from the poker session the winner of approximately $500, which was around $500 better than usual. If my mental tally was correct, I was nearly $35 ahead of the

11

game, which had been running now for a little more than three years. My uncanny skill as a card player still seemed no viable substitute for industriousness, thrift, and pluck—character traits that somehow had eluded me over the years.

Because there was still nothing to do and time to waste I went into the bathroom, admired the lime green fixtures, brushed my teeth, and inspected my gums, which were receding, a dentist had recently told me, at a normally healthy pace. I wondered what that was: a centimeter a year? Less? Probably more. A little depressed by my inspection and not at all confident that the Coulter Museum served a preluncheon drink, I went down to the lobby and into the bar and ordered a martini. It was half-past noon, but the bar was barely a fourth full. Only the truly thirsty seemed willing to brave the Capital's noonday sun.

When Amos Woodrow Coulter died unexpectedly in 1964 from infectious hepatitis at the age of 51, unmarried and alone, he left most of his estimated $500 million fortune to several foundations and the Federal government, noting in his will that the government "will probably get it anyway," but including the carefully drawn provision that the money be used to build a gallery or museum in Washington to house his vast art collection and to acquire "other works of merit, interest, worth, and significance as they appear on the world market."

Coulter had made his fortune in electronics, and most of the gadgets that his firm patented and manufactured were snapped up by the government to guide its missiles and steer its rockets to the moon and beyond. When not making money, Coulter and his extremely knowledgeable agents toured the world and spent it on art in wholesale lots when possible, on individual works when not. His formal education had been ended by the depression of the thirties when he was a sophomore at Texas Christian University but even then possessed by a love for art in all its forms. There were those who claimed that Amos Coulter never married because he never found a woman who was willing to let him hang her on a wall. In any event, his eye for art more than matched his passion. He made his first purchase, a Modigliani, in 1946, shortly after he made his first million. From then, until the time of his death, he spent lavishly and bought shrewdly on a rising market. When he died, his collection, exclusive of his other holdings and interests, was conservatively valued at $200 million.

Coulter himself designed the museum that was to bear his name and it stood now just off Independence Avenue on several acres of ground formerly occupied by "temporary" World War I buildings that had been hastily thrown up in 1917 and were still in use almost a half century later. An act of Congress in 1965 had donated the land for the museum and, although in existence for only a few years, it was already acknowledged, with a few carping exceptions, as one of the finest in the world. Those who didn't like it didn't like the Guggenheim either.

It was an impressive building in a city of impressive buildings. Although only five stories high it still managed to soar a little, and if it didn't command awe, it at least earned admiration and respect. Built of Italian marble and textured concrete, it covered almost a block and somehow created the atmosphere of a friendly gallery instead of a municipal jail and it seemed to beckon the passer-by to come in and look around. I admired it while the cab made its approach, and when inside a guard informed me that Mrs. Wingo's office was on the fifth floor and that the elevators were just to my left. On the fifth floor a discreet sign pointed the way to the director's office and when I walked in a young Negro girl looked up from her typewriter, smiled, and wanted to know if I was Mr. St. Ives. When I said that I was she said that Mrs. Wingo was expecting me.

13

Mrs. Frances Wingo, director of the Coulter Museum, sat behind a boomerang-shaped desk of inlaid wood that had nothing on it other than a pair of rather hideous African statues about nine inches tall and a telephone console that seemed to have at least three dozen buttons. Behind her, to the east, a window provided a view of the Capitol building, which looked no more real than it does in those movies about Washington where it always seems to be just across the street from every man's office, even if he works in the basement of the Pentagon out in Virginia. It was a large room, nicely carpeted, about the size of that awarded to an under-secretary of State or the majority whip in the House of Representatives. There was even a fireplace at one end with some club chairs and a couch grouped around it. There were a number of paintings on the cork-lined walls and I recognized a Klee and thought it a shame that it was tucked away out of public view.

"I rotate the paintings in here every week, Mr. St. Ives," said Frances Wingo, the mind reader. "None is kept from public view. Do sit down."

I sat in something comfortable that was made out of down-stuffed leather and wood. There was no ashtray in sight, but Frances Wingo opened a drawer and placed a blue, oblong ceramic dish in front of me. I decided not to smoke. She was a little over or a little under thirty, and rather tall unless she was sitting on a couple of pillows. She wore a dark brown dress of some nubby weave and that slightly defensive expression that most female executives wear who have reached the top before they are thirty-five. After that, the expression usually hardens into grim resolve. She had cut her hair short, perhaps too short, and for a moment I thought that she might be a practicing dyke, but her eyes were too soft and brown and large, although it may have been that she was having trouble with her thyroids. Her nose tipped up slightly and she hadn't bothered to disguise the freckles that were sprinkled across its bridge. Her mouth was wide, but not too wide, and it was hard to tell whether she wore lipstick. Frances Wingo, I decided, was a long way from being beautiful, but she had a face you could remember with pleasure and it probably looked the same at breakfast as it did over cocktails.

"You come highly recommended," she said.

"By whom?"

"By your Mr. Greene and by whoever stole the shield."

"I understand that they asked for me."

"Not asked," she said. "Insisted."

"I'm not sure that I'm flattered."

She opened a desk drawer and took out a yellow, unsharpened pencil and absently began to tap its eraser against the top of her desk. "Senator Kehoel on our executive committee also had some nice things to say about you."

"That's because I wrote some nice things about him," I said. "A long time ago."

"Four years ago," she said, still tapping away with the pencil. "Just before your paper folded. I'm surprised that you're no longer writing; you had an interesting style."

"Not enough newspapers to go around; at least not in New York."

"And elsewhere?"

"Elsewhere thinks I'm too expensive."

She glanced at a watch that she wore on her right wrist. "The others should be in the dining room. You can save your questions until after lunch. All right?"

"Fine."

We rose and she was as tall as I expected, nearly five-eight or -nine. The loosely cut brown dress failed to disguise her figure, but she probably knew that and used it for business purposes. I followed her across the room to the door and admired the sway of her hips and the curve of her calves, which, I was pleased to note, were encased in nylon and not in cotton webbing or linsey-woolsey. When it comes to women's clothes I seem to have decidedly reactionary tendencies, but it's something I've been told that I may grow out of.

Frances Wingo paused at the door and looked at me with a kind of flickering interest, as if I were a slightly audacious watercolor that, while amusing perhaps, was not something one would purchase.

"Tell me something, Mr. St. Ives," she said.

"What?"

"When you fill in that blank on your income-tax form which asks for occupation, what do you put down?"

"Go-between."

"And that's really what you are?"

"Yes," I said. "That's really what I am."

It had all started casually enough four years back, just before the newspaper that I worked for folded, the victim of a prolonged strike, an unworkable merger, a forgettable new name, and rotten management. I wrote a feature five days a week about those New Yorkers of high, middle, and low estate who caught my fancy, and because I have a fairly good ear, a high-school course in shorthand, and a careless personality (my ex-wife called it permissive, but then she was always up on the latest clichés), the stories were usually well received. It also caused me to become acquainted with a large collection of oddballs and once there was even talk of syndication, but nothing ever came of it.

My new career began when a client of Myron Greene's was robbed of $196,000 worth of jewelry (the insurance company's reluctant estimate) and the thief let it be known that he was willing to sell it all back for a mere $40,000 provided that I served as the intermediary, or go-between. "I read his colyum," the thief had told Myron Greene over the phone. "The guy don't give a shit about nothing."

16

Myron Greene and a representative of the insurance company approached me, and I agreed to serve as go-between provided that I could write about it once the negotiations were concluded. The man from the insurance company balked at that because he seemed to feel that a dose of clap was preferable to publicity. "After all, St. Ives," he had said, "we certainly don't want you to write a primer on extortion."

Eventually he agreed because he didn't have much choice, and on the day of the transaction I hung around nine different public phone booths where I received instructions from the thief. The exchange was finally made at 3 A.M. on a subway headed for Coney Island. The thief got his money; I got the jewelry. The affair provided me with a couple of good features and it even got mentioned in the press section of *Newsweek*. I was just about to suggest a raise when the notice went up on the city room's bulletin board that as of 6 P.M. that very day, the newspaper no longer existed.

They caught the thief, a small-timer named Albert Fontaine, three weeks later in Miami Beach where he was spending too much money on the wrong people. I visited him in the Tombs once after extradition because I had nothing better to do. He wanted to know if I was going to write him up in my "colyum."

"The paper folded, Al," I said.

"That's a goddamned shame," Fontaine said, and then, because he wanted to say something else, something nice, I suppose, he said, "You know something, I thought you wrote real good." They finally gave Albert Fontaine six years.

My wife and I, perfectly mismatched as if by computer, parted shortly thereafter on a pleasantly acrimonious note and just as the severance pay was running out, I received another call from Myron Greene, the lawyer. He wanted me to serve as a go-between again.

"Your clients seem to have a lot of trouble," I said.

"Well, it's not really *my* client. It's the client of a friend of mine who remembers how you handled the other thing."

"What is it?" I said. "More jewelry?"

"Not exactly. It's a little more serious than that."

"How much more?"

"Well, it's a kidnaping."

"No thanks."

Myron Greene's asthma got worse. I could hear him wheeze over the phone. "Uh—there may be a slight risk involved."

"That's why I said no."

"My friend's client is perfectly willing to compensate you, of course."

"How much is a slight risk worth to him?"

"Say ten thousand dollars?"

"Nobody pays that much for a slight risk."

"Well, there's—"

"Hold on," I said. I thought a moment and then asked: "How much do you charge for divorces?"

"I've never handled a divorce," Myron Greene said, a little stiffly, I thought.

"Well, if you did, how much would you charge?"

"I don't really know, there's—"

"Get me a divorce *and* the ten thousand and I'll do it."

It was Myron Greene's turn to think. "All right," he said after a few moments. "Can you be at my office at five?"

Despite the high-priced and perfectly sound advice of the attorney who was Myron Greene's friend, the family of the kidnap victim refused to call in either the New York police or the FBI. Instead, they insisted on following the kidnapers' instructions exactly. The instructions weren't very innovative. They had me drop a satchel stuffed with $100,000 in used ten- and twenty-dollar bills along a lonely stretch of New Jersey farm road at 3:30 in the morning. I then drove for three minutes at exactly 20 miles an hour until my headlights picked up the family's heir, a 20-year-old youth who was staggering down the center of the road, his hands tied behind him. He was also completely hysterical.

The story never made the papers, but it got around, and the police and even the FBI started to drop in on me at odd hours. When they began to mention the penalty for neglecting to report a felony, I called Myron Greene who called his friend who called his wealthy client. The client presumably called the mayor or the governor or God, and the visits from the FBI and the police stopped.

The third time that I heard from Myron Greene was four months later just as the ten thousand dollars was nearing its end, the victim of my profligate ways and a visit from a polite but firm representative of the Internal Revenue Service. This time Myron Greene suggested that we enter into an agreement whereby he would negotiate my fee in exchange for ten percent of whatever it was.

"In other words you want ten percent of my ten percent," I said.

"It would be decidedly advantageous to you," Myron Greene said.

"I didn't think you would walk across the street for a thousand-dollar fee."

He paused and I listened to his asthma for a while. "It's not the fee really," he said. "It's not that at all. It's simply that I find such proceedings fascinating." He sighed a little, a wheezy sort of a sigh. "I really should have been a criminal lawyer."

"It would just make your asthma worse."

I decided that Myron Greene could throw in a few more services if he wanted to be a go-between's agent, so we negotiated at length in his Madison Avenue offices. Finally, he agreed to accept my power of attorney and to perform such onerous chores as filing my quarterly income-tax statements on time, paying my bills, keeping my alimony payments current, and even maintaining my checkbook in some kind of order. His secretary, a forty-five-year-old dynamo whom Myron Greene called Spivack, would do the work and the lawyer would get ten percent of whatever fees came my way and the pleasure of being, vicariously at least, in the company of thieves.

During the four years that followed I found that it was not a vocation or profession that needed advertising. The lawyers and the thieves and the insurance companies and even the cops spread the word that I could be trusted to follow instructions and that I was as honest as could be reasonably expected. Nearly all of the assignments came through Myron Greene, four or five or six a year, and they netted me a satisfactory if not gaudy living, even after the alimony payments were dispatched once a month.

Most of the thieves eventually got caught, but some never did—the kidnapers, for example—and those who did wind up in jail always gave me a warm recommendation to anyone who cared to listen. Sometimes I visited them or sent cigarettes and magazines. I felt that it was the least I could do to encourage the source of my income.

"Yours must be a curious sort of life, Mr. St. Ives," Frances Wingo said as we walked down the hall to the museum's executive dining room. "I don't believe I've ever met a professional go-between before."

"Few people do until they need one."

"Do you have much competition?" she said.

"No," I said. "Only my better judgment."

3

I knew two of the three men who stood at the small bar at the far end of the dining room. The tall, fragile one with the salt and pepper forelock that kept flopping down into his melancholy eyes was Senator Augustus Kehoel (pronounced "curl" for some reason) of Ohio, who was the delight of the political cartoonists. They always made him look like a grief-stricken sheep dog. At twenty-four and just out of the World War II army with something of a hero's record, he had married into a car-wax fortune and over the years had spent goodly chunk of it getting himself elected to the state legislature, the U.S. House of Representatives, and finally to the Senate. It was as high as he would ever go although he once had hinted to me of some yearning to be vice-president, which only demonstrated that he was a reasonable man of limited ambition.

Next to him, with a carefully manicured hand in

firm control of a double martini, was Lawrence Igna-
tius Teague, president of the million-member Aluminum Workers of America (AFL-CIO), and pink of
cheek and white of hair. I wondered if he still used a
blue rinse. During an internal union scrap five or six
years before, one of his dissident staff members had
sneaked us both into Teague's suite at the Waldorf,
ushered me into a bathroom, and grimly displayed a
bottle of blue rinse that he swore the labor leader
used faithfully, but I didn't think it was anything to
hang a man for.

"You know Senator Kehoel," Mrs. Wingo said.

"Senator."

"Good to see you, Phil," he said, and we shook
hands.

"And Lawrence Teague."

"Hello, Larry."

"Wonderful to see you, Phil," he said, putting his
glass down and grabbing my right hand with both of
his. "Wonderful." It really wasn't, but this was called
the Teague touch and I suppose it had helped him to
stay in office for more than two decades at sixty thousand a year plus an unlimited expense account. For all
I knew, he was worth it.

I told him that I thought it was wonderful, too, and
then turned to the third man at the bar who stood
quietly, a seemingly untouched drink at his elbow,
and separated by far more than space from the senator
and the union president. Only his green eyes moved
as I turned to him. They settled first on my face, then
traveled down to take in and assess my tie, jacket,
trousers, and shoes, and finally rose again to fix themselves on a spot an inch or so above my left eyebrow.
Somehow I resisted the impulse to finger the spot to
find out how deep the hole went.

"And the chairman of our executive committee,"
Frances Wingo was saying, "Winfield Spencer. Mr.
Spencer, Mr. St. Ives."

When Spencer moved, he seemed to do so reluctantly, as if it cost him a great deal of effort. He extended his right hand and I accepted it. Although not at all keen on meaty handshakes, I did expect something more than I got from Winfield Spencer, who held his own hand perfectly still while I either pressed or massaged or fondled it, I'm still not quite sure which, but he didn't seem to care much for whatever I was doing and neither did I, so I dropped it as soon as I could.

"Mr. Spencer," I said.

"St. Ives," he murmured, lowered his gaze, turned quickly, rested his elbows on the bar, and began a careful study of the labels on the bottles behind it.

Only Winfield Spencer's name would cause you to look at him twice if you were interested in money and three times if you were concerned with power. Even in August he wore a three-piece gray worsted suit that could have been tailored this year or in 1939; it was that kind of material and that kind of cut. His hair was pewter gray and it looked as if he trimmed it himself, but had botched the job. He had no sideburns and the back of his neck was irregularly shaved an inch or so above a frayed white collar displaying a few threads that the manicure scissors had missed.

Over the years Spencer seemed to have created a face for himself that was at once both shy and forbidding. It was an ugly face, purposely ugly, I thought, because the mouth was always pursed, the forehead was always frowned, and the chin, a little small by some standards, was always thrust out in an aggressively unpleasant manner. The clip-on maroon bow tie that he wore beneath it didn't help things any either.

I found it difficult to believe that Winfield Spencer had once shot down nine Messerschmitts for the Royal Canadian Air Force. I found it even more difficult to believe that he was either the fifth- or sixth-richest man in the nation.

The Spencer fortune had been founded in the

1850's on Pennsylvania coal. It was augmented by Colorado gold and silver, Montana copper, some short-line railroads, and later by Texas, Oklahoma, and California oil, and much later by Utah uranium. It was now buttressed by refineries, a fleet of tankers, and a Washington bank whose deposits, including the considerable pension funds from Teague's aluminum workers, had been used to buy into some of the nation's most profitable businesses; and Spencer's bank made sure that these businesses continued to be profitable by a complicated, almost unravelable tangle of interlocking directorates.

Just out of Princeton in 1939, Spencer had joined the Canadian air force in September and got nine of his own before he was shot down over the Channel in the late summer of 1942. He was invalided back to the States that fall because of injuries, some said, while others claimed that he was eased out because of psychological reasons.

Since then Spencer had devoted himself to anonymity, the family fortune, and art. It was art that had brought him and Amos Coulter together. In the early 1950's a Matisse had been auctioned in London by Sotheby's. Spencer's agents had been instructed to buy it; Amos Coulter was on hand to do his own bidding. But Coulter's new fortune proved no match for Spencer's older and considerably larger bankroll. Spencer got the Matisse and when informed how high Amos Coulter had bid for it, he had had the picture crated and sent to Coulter without any notice, not even a card.

The two men subsequently became friends, or close acquaintances at any rate, since Spencer was said to have no friends. Coulter was one of the three dozen or so persons who had been invited to view the Spencer collection, which was carefully housed and guarded in a private gallery built on his plantation near Warrenton, Virginia, and which supposedly contained the world's finest collection of postimpressionists. But de-

24

spite the fact that he had been as close to Amos Coulter as he had ever been to anyone, it still took three personal phone calls from the President himself before Winfield Spencer agreed to serve as chairman of the Coulter Museum's executive committee.

Some of this went through my mind as I stood at the bar between the senator and the labor leader and half listened as they gossiped about the state of the union, and some of it I looked up later. Frances Wingo now stood at Spencer's left, talking to him in a low voice while he continued his study of the labels on the bottles behind the bar. When the bartender slid my drink over to me I turned to Senator Kehoel.

"Good session?" I asked.

"Rotten," he said. "But considering what we now have in the White House it was better than I expected."

"Give him time," Teague said.

"Why?"

Teague patted a stray lock of silvery hair into place while he thought up an answer. "He has good people around him," he said.

"So did Caesar," the senator said.

"Think I have time for one more of these?" Teague said, looking sadly into his empty martini glass.

"I don't know," the senator said. "You'll have to ask God."

As if on cue, God, or Winfield Spencer, turned from Frances Wingo and said, "I think we should start." He walked slowly over to the carefully set table and took the chair at its head, not waiting for Frances Wingo. I noticed that Spencer moved with a slight limp. Lawrence Teague bustled over to Mrs. Wingo and held her chair, which was on Spencer's left. I sat next to her and the senator and Teague sat across from us.

Lunch, for four of us at least, was ordinary but eatable: grilled double-cut lamb chops, fresh peas, new potatoes, and salad. The bartender, who doubled as waiter, served it skillfully enough, but seemed to

25

wince when he got around to Spencer, whose plate contained two hard-boiled eggs and six soda crackers, which he grimly washed down with a glass of buttermilk.

There was little conversation during the meal. Spencer ate slowly and when finished he brushed a few cracker crumbs from his vest and tapped a forefinger softly on the tablecloth. I assumed that he was calling the meeting to order. He was.

"When the coffee is served, we'll begin," he said, staring into his now empty plate. The dishes were cleared away, the coffee was promptly served, and I lit a cigarette. No one else smoked.

Spencer looked up from his plate and his green eyes seemed to fasten on some imaginary guest at the end of the table. From the tone of Spencer's voice, the imaginary guest was apparently none too bright. "The museum suffered a theft on Friday night. That is the reason for this meeting. Mrs. Wingo will now give us a detailed report. Do not ask questions until she is finished." With that he dropped his eyes back to the spot where his plate containing the two hard-boiled eggs and six soda crackers had rested. He didn't look up until Frances Wingo stopped talking. She had quite a bit to say and she said it well.

"I'll start at the beginning," she said. "As all of you know, with the possible exception of Mr. St. Ives, we consider ourselves extremely fortunate to have secured what is known as the Pan-African collection. In truth it is somewhat misnamed because all of it comes from south of the Sahara, but even so it represents the finest collection of black African art ever assembled. Most of the pieces are considered national treasures and have never before been exhibited outside their respective countries. I will not attempt to catalogue all of the pieces that are of extreme value, or even priceless because of their historical worth, but only point out that none of them exceeds the shield of Komporeen in beauty, historical significance, value, and, unfortunately, political importance. The shield, of course, was stolen last Friday night."

She paused for a sip of water. "The shield of Komporeen was first mentioned by an anonymous Portuguese pilot who wrote of it in his account of his explorations of the west coast of Africa in 1539. He described it as hanging behind the throne of the Odo, or natural ruler of Komporeen, and noted that it was, as he wrote, 'the subject of much veneration.' Komporeen, of course, is the former name for what is now known as the Republic of Jandola, which secured its independence from the British in 1958. It was not until the 1870's that the shield of Komporeen was mentioned again. Sir William Cranville wrote a detailed description of it in what came to be known as the Cranville Report. He mistakenly described the shield as being of 'obvious Portuguese derivation, but nevertheless of exquisite workmanship.' Another near quote was when he wrote that 'the native leaders insist that it portrays their history from ancient times, but I regard this as highly improbable.'"

Once again Frances Wingo sipped some water. "In 1910," she went on, "the first detailed report on the shield was contained in a monograph privately published in London by Jonathon Twill, the archeologist. He described it as being cast by the 'lost wax' method, which was first used by the people of the Nile. He measured and weighed the shield and found it to weigh 68 pounds and to measure 39 inches in diameter. He also noted that it was constantly guarded and for the first time reported its real significance.

"Winston wrote that the Komporeeneans believed that whoever possessed the shield was empowered to rule the nation. He also mentioned that possession of the shield had been the cause of what he described as 'innumerable intertribal wars.'

"In the late 1940's a special British commission was appointed to make a thorough investigation of the shield of Komporeen. Although it was unable to interpret the meaning of the bas-relief figures which stem from its center in a series of ever-widening concentric circles, it was able to establish the approximate age. The shield of Komporeen was judged to have been cast in the ninth century. As such, it is far older than the bronzes and brasses of Ife and Benin in Nigeria.

"The shield of Komporeen was on display in the Jandolaean National Museum in Brefu, the second-largest city in the republic. It was only with the greatest reluctance that the Jandolaean government agreed to permit the shield to become part of the Pan-African Exhibition. They did so, frankly, because of their intense feeling of nationalism, which made them want to boast, understandably enough, I suppose, of their past civilization, which was capable of producing such a magnificent work of art at a time when Europe was emerging from its dark ages."

Again she paused, sipped some more water, and looked at Spencer. "I hope I'm not taking too much time," she said.

"Go on," Spencer said.

"The Pan-African Exhibit has now been on tour for nearly a year. During this time a revolution has broken out in Jandola, as I'm sure you know. Both the Federal government of Jandola and the breakaway province which has adopted the ancient name of Komporeen claim the shield as their own. Unfortunately, the shield has become a primary symbol in the civil war and both sides attach an extraordinary amount of significance to its possession. The U.S. has no diplomatic relations with the breakaway nation of Komporeen. Jandola, for the moment, is content to let the shield remain in the U.S. for obvious political and propaganda purposes. It was my unpleasant task to inform their embassy that it had been stolen. I might add that the reverberations from their embassy, as well as from our State Department, can only be described as severe.

"The theft of the shield was discovered at twelve

twenty-five Friday morning. The Metropolitan Police were immediately notified, as was I. Shortly thereafter I called Mr. Spencer and then the Jandolaean Embassy. Because of the shield's unique political significance, it was agreed that news of the theft would not be released. After investigating, the police concluded that the theft was an inside job. You are aware that the museum contains the most sophisticated electronic warning and alarm devices available. Mr. Amos Coulter designed some of them himself. A theft by forced entry is virtually impossible. To bear out the inside-job theory one of the guards assigned to the Pan-African Exhibition failed to report to work the following afternoon. His name is John Sackett and police have been unable to locate him. He has been employed by the museum for nearly eight months."

Frances Wingo needed another sip of water. "Last Friday, at 11:15 in the morning, I received a call from a man who seemed to be speaking with a voice that he artificially muffled. He informed me that the shield would be returned in exchange for the sum of $250,000. He then insisted that Mr. St. Ives here was to serve as the intermediary, or go-between. He gave me the name of Mr. St. Ives' attorney in New York, said that more details would be forthcoming, and then hung up. I immediately called the police, told them what had happened, and then called Mr. Spencer. He authorized me to call Mr. Myron Greene, who is Mr. St. Ives' attorney, and to arrange this meeting of the executive committee and Mr. St. Ives. I have heard no more from the man who demanded the $250,000."

She stopped again and took another sip of water. I expected her to go on, but she remained silent and the silence lasted almost thirty seconds until Spencer spoke.

"I recommend that we pay the $250,000—plus Mr. St. Ives' fee, which is, I'm informed, ten percent." He addressed his remarks once again to the imaginary guest at the end of the table.

"We are responsible, I suppose," Senator Kehoel said.

"What about insurance?" Teague said.

"We're covered," Spencer said.

"So it's all right then," Teague said.

It was the wrong thing to say. Spencer shifted his green gaze from the imaginary guest to Teague. "No," he said, "it is not all right. This museum has suffered the theft of a priceless, irreplaceable work of art, one that threatens to cause an international incident. Furthermore, the museum's reputation for security has been damaged, perhaps irreparably. No, Mr. Teague, it is not all right."

Senator Kehoel hurried to say something while the flush rose in Teague's face. "Perhaps we should first determine whether Mr. St. Ives is willing to serve as intermediary. Are you?"

"Yes," I said. "I suppose I am."

"And to help apprehend the thieves?" Spencer asked.

"I'm afraid that's not my job," I said.

"Twenty-five thousand dollars should buy something more than a messenger boy," Spencer said.

"It does," I said. "It buys you a link to the shield, something you don't have right now. All you've got is a phone call from a muffled voice and you really don't know if it's for real or a hoax. But you've already made your decision: you've decided that you want the shield returned more than you want the thieves caught and you're willing to pay a quarter of a million dollars for what you want. Of course, what you'd really like is to get the shield back and the thieves caught at the same time. It's an understandable reaction. Just about everyone would have it, but it doesn't work that way."

Spencer was once more staring at the spot an inch or so above my left eyebrow. "How does it work, Mr. St. Ives?" he said.

"You pay me twenty-five thousand dollars to make sure that you don't pay a quarter of a million for nothing. It's happened before, of course, especially in kidnaping cases where the ransom has been paid and the kidnap victim has been killed. The go-between business is really a matter of trust. You trust me with a quarter of a million in cash because you believe I won't part with it until I'm convinced that I can get the shield back. The thieves trust me because they're convinced that they won't wind up with a suitcase full of cut-up newspaper and a couple of hundred cops popping up from behind the bushes. And the cops trust me because they know that I'll give them every scrap of information about the thieves that I get— once the shield is returned. And finally, the twenty-five thousand pays me for whatever risk I take. There's always the chance that I'll wind up with a bullet in my back, you with nothing, and the thieves with a quarter of a million and an African shield that they can hang up in the living room next to the *Playboy* calendar."

"And that's as far as your services go?" Frances Wingo said.

"Yes," I said. "That's as far as they go and I think it's far enough considering the risk involved. If what you think you need is a little derring-do, someone who'll meet the thieves at the old mill at midnight, whip out his Smith & Wesson, and cart them, a 50-pound suitcase full of money, and a 68-pound shield down to the nearest precinct station, then I'm not a candidate for the job. I'm not even a dark horse."

"That could be the reason that the thieves insist that you serve as go-between, Mr. St. Ives," Spencer said, still fascinated by the spot on my forehead. "You must have something of a reputation for caution."

"Some might call it cowardice," I said.

"Yes," Spencer said, "I suppose that some might." He shifted his gaze from my forehead to the imaginary guest at the end of the table. "I recommend that we engage Mr. St. Ives to carry out the negotiations for the return of the shield. Senator?"

Senator Kehoel nodded. "I agree."

"Mr. Teague?" Spencer said.

"He has my vote," Teague said.

"Then it's agreed," Spencer said. "You will accept the assignment, Mr. St. Ives?"

"Yes," I said, "provided you accept the conditions I've mentioned."

"They are acceptable," Spencer said. "Is a deposit or a retainer the usual form?"

"One half," I said.

"Will you see to it, Mrs. Wingo?" he said.

"Of course," she said.

"Now that you're the museum's official go-between," Spencer said, "what will be your first move?"

"I'll go back to New York and wait for someone to call or write me a letter or send a telegram."

"You won't remain here in Washington?"

"When whoever stole the shield asked for me, they knew that I lived in New York, so I assume that's where they'll get in touch with me."

"You think the exchange will be made there, Phil?" Teague said.

"It could be," I said. "There or here or Kansas City or Miami. They might be moving around."

Spencer got up slowly from the table. "You'll keep us informed through Mrs. Wingo," he said.

"Yes."

As the rest of us began to rise the bartender-waiter hurried over with a telephone. "It's for you, Mrs. Wingo," he said. "Your secretary says it's important." She nodded and he plugged the phone into a jack underneath the table.

After she said hello she said, "Yes, Lieutenant," and then she listened for several moments. Finally she said, "I'm sorry to hear that, but thank you for calling." She hung up the phone and the waiter unplugged it and took it away.

"That was Lieutenant Demeter of the Metropolitan Police Robbery Squad," she said. "Two children playing in Rock Creek Park discovered the body of a dead man. He'd been shot. He was identified as John Sackett, the guard who didn't show up for work Friday morning."

4

When the young Negro secretary with the pleasant
smile brought the machine-signed check in, Frances
Wingo merely glanced at it and then pushed it across
her desk to me with the eraser of the unsharpened
yellow pencil that she kept bouncing against the inlaid wood.

"You may still back out, right?" she said as I put the
check away in my wallet.

"I've been thinking about it."

"Because of what happened to the guard?"

"It did give me a new perspective."

"The obvious one?"

"Obvious to me anyway."

"You mean whoever killed the guard stole the
shield?"

"That's one."

"What's two?"

"That it was all a carefully planned operation,
which suggests professionals."

Frances Wingo tapped the eraser some more. "They had three months to work it out."

"Why three months?"

"Because that's when we first knew that we were going to get the exhibition. Up until then, we weren't sure."

"And you announced it then?"

"Yes," she said. "It made quite a nice splash."

"Did the shield get more publicity or attention than any other piece?"

"The Jandolaean Embassy saw to that."

"Then whoever stole it had three whole months to find themselves an accomplice," I said. "You can do a lot of persuading in three months."

Frances Wingo quit tapping the pencil and I almost thanked her. "Why do you think they killed the guard—provided they killed him?" she said.

I shrugged. "Probably to save money and to keep him from talking. Or maybe he planned the whole thing himself and someone got greedy, but that seems a little farfetched."

"But the murder hasn't yet changed your mind?"

"Not yet."

"You mean it could later?"

"At any time."

Frances Wingo didn't like that so she started tapping the eraser on her desk again. "You didn't mention that before."

"An oversight," I said.

"I thought that's what you were being paid for, to take such risks."

"No. You're paying me to get the shield back, not to run risks. My principal problem is to arrange the transaction so that the risks are minimized. If I find that I can't do that, then I'll back out."

She looked at me for a long moment. "You're not exactly the boy adventurer, are you?"

"Not exactly," I said, but the topic was beginning to bore me so I asked her a question. "What do I do if I suddenly find that I need a quarter of a million dollars in relatively small bills at three o'clock tomorrow afternoon in Pittsburgh?"

She didn't hesitate or stop tapping the eraser. "You call me," she said. "Mr. Spencer will either arrange for a corresponding bank to supply the money or it will be flown to you by private plane from Washington."

"To wherever I need it?"

"To wherever you need it. Anything else?"

"A couple of things. If you get any more calls from the man with the muffled voice, tell him he can reach me at the Madison until nine in the morning; after that I'll be at my place in New York." I gave her the number and she stopped tapping the pencil long enough to write it down on a buff-colored pad.

"All right," she said. "What else?"

"The last item. If you're free this evening, you might drop by the Madison and I'll buy you a drink."

She leaned back in her chair and looked at me speculatively. This time I was no longer a slightly audacious watercolor; I was a forgery trying to pass as an old master and not a very good forgery at that.

"Don't you think my husband might object, Mr. St. Ives?"

"No," I said, "because I don't think you're married, at least not any more."

"Why not?"

"You just don't look married."

She rose then and there was nothing else for me to do but rise with her. "If you need any more information about the shield, Mr. St. Ives, please feel free to call at any time."

"If you change your mind, the offer for the drink still stands," I said.

She looked down at her desk, picked up the yellow pencil, and began to tap the eraser against the wood. "Thank you, but I don't think so."

At the door I paused and looked back. I don't know

36

why I bothered because I really didn't care whether I bought her a drink. "But you're not married, are you?"

"No, Mr. St. Ives," she said, "I'm not. Not any more. My husband died in an auto accident four weeks ago."

It had warmed up a little, I noticed, as I stood outside the museum and vainly waited for the miracle of a cruising cab. I stood in the shade of a telephone pole, and wondered what the temperature was in Leadville and San Francisco and Nome and some other fine places. After a quarter of an hour or so a cab came along with its windows rolled up, which meant that it was either air-conditioned or the driver had gone mad. It was twenty degrees cooler inside and I asked to be driven to police headquarters.

"Wait a minute," the driver said, and pointed at his radio, which was blasting an acid rock number so loud that the speaker vibrated.

"Your song?" I said.

"No, man, the temperature's coming on."

We waited, not moving, until the number was nearly through and then the disk jockey's voice came on, crackling hard over the fading dissonance: "Now it *is* warm out there. Man down at the weather bureau says it's one hundred and two, that's t-w-o, degrees right here in the nation's Capital. That's uh-one-uh-oh-uh-two degrees and Mr. Weatherman says that's the all-time record for this August date. So why don't you lean back, grab something tall and cool—to drink, I mean—and listen to—" The driver switched it off and looked at his watch.

"If it don't get no hotter, I won," he said.

"Won what?"

"The weather pool. I had a hundred and two at 3 P.M. Twenty-five-dollar pool."

"Let's hope you won. Now how about the police station?"

He turned to look at me then, a dark brown man with his hair worn natural bush, I suppose, and the blackest pair of sunglasses over his eyes that I'd ever seen.

"Now we've got a lot of police stations," he said. "We've got the Park Police and the Capital Police and the Metropolitan Police and we've got fourteen precinct police stations plus the harbor unit down on Main Avenue and that's still not counting the FBI and the CIA out in Virginia. Just make your choice and I'll be happy to take you to any one of them."

"Let's try the Metropolitan Police headquarters," I said. "If that doesn't work out, I'll give the rest of them a go."

The cab moved away from the curb with something of a racing start. "The Metropolitan Police headquarters is located at 300 Indiana Avenue," the driver said. "A very nice neighborhood out of the high-rent district and within easy walking distance of the Capitol and a lousy sixty-five-cent ride from here."

It was a brief ride and the driver kept up his running commentary until we pulled up before a large, six-story granite building whose architectural style leaned toward Midwestern municipal. "How much?" I said.

"Like I said, sixty-five cents unless you're a big spender from out of town."

"You figured it out after all," I said, and gave him a dollar.

"Thank you, my good man, and I hope you have a pleasant visit with the friendlies."

"And I hope you win the pool."

Inside there was the usual number of people who had reason to come calling on the police at three o'clock in the afternoon. They avoided each other's eyes as they waited before the bank of four elevators that would take them up to talk to someone with a badge about something that had turned out differently from what they had expected. About something that had turned out wrong.

The halls of the building, which also seemed to contain the city's tax division, were covered with black marble that ran halfway up the wall and then turned into pale green plaster. The floors were covered with black and white speckled marble and it all seemed solid and secure and as if it were meant to last for a long time. A directory said that the robbery squad was on the third floor so I took one of the elevators up and when I emerged the first thing that I saw on the right was a brown shield about eighteen inches high with gold lettering that read ROBBERY SQUAD. The door was open and I walked into a small waiting area that was bounded by frosted glass and plywood partitions. A worn brown bench, something like a pew in an old church whose building fund suffered a deficit, was placed against one of the walls, apparently for the use of robber and victim alike. At the left was a door and a window that was very much like a bank teller's cage without the bars. I approached the window and a man in a white shirt, blue tie, and a holstered gun under his left arm wanted to know if he could help me.

"I'd like to see Lieutenant Demeter," I said.

"Your name?"

"Philip St. Ives."

"How do you spell it?"

I spelled it for him, he wrote it down, and disappeared. In a few moments he was back. He opened the door at his right and motioned me through. "This way," he said. I followed him into a room that contained some desks, chairs, and telephones. He pointed to a door at the far end of the room. "Right through there," he said. I went through that door into a smaller room that contained two gray metal desks, some matching chairs, and two men in shirt sleeves who sat behind the desks. There was one window, but the venetian blind was lowered and I couldn't tell whether they had a view of the Capitol.

"Lieutenant Demeter?" I said.

The older of the two men looked up from a sheet of paper he was reading. He was in no hurry. "I'm Demeter," he said. "What's your problem?"

"I'm Philip St. Ives," I said. "I've been hired by the Coulter Museum to buy the shield back from whoever stole it."

Demeter carefully put the paper he had been reading in the exact center of his desk, leaned back in his chair, rested his hands on its arms, and inspected me with small, black beanlike eyes that darted around my face until they finally decided to settle on my nose. He was built like a stubby tube, I noticed, as thick as he was wide. Meaty shoulders sloped abruptly from the size-seventeen neck that supported a big-jawed head which had a nice crop of black hair that looked as if it had been wet-combed in a vain attempt to get a few of the curls out. His jumbo nose, all angles and flaring, hairy nostrils, jutted out over a wide mouth with thin red lips. He also had a carefully trimmed mustache that would have done credit to Ronald Colman if one could remember back that far. Lieutenant Demeter could; he was at least forty; maybe even forty-five.

"You look hot," he said. "You're sweating. Take a chair."

I took a chair and, still looking at me, or at least at my nose, he said, "Call the Wingo woman at the Coulter Museum. See if she's got a St. what?"

"Ives," I said.

"See if she's got a St. Ives working for her."

The other man in shirt sleeves picked up his phone and dialed a number. He was younger than Demeter, somewhere in his early thirties, and he also had curly hair, but it was blond, and his eyes were blue. He didn't wear a mustache under his snub nose, which was peeling a little from sunburn, so I decided that Demeter might not be his idol.

When the younger man got through dialing, he said,

"This is Sergeant Fastnaught, Mrs. Wingo. We have a party here who says he's been hired by the museum in connection with the stolen shield." He paused. "What's your first name, mister?" he said to me.

"Philip."

"That's right," Fastnaught said into the phone. "Philip St. Ives...I see...thank you, Mrs. Wingo." He hung up the phone, leaned back in his chair, and locked his hands behind his head. "She said that they hired him this afternoon."

Demeter nodded, still fascinated by my nose. "We get a lot of nuts in here," he said. "You got any identification?"

I took out my wallet and handed over a New York driver's license, which he read all the way through before handing it back.

"He's who he says he is," Demeter said to Sergeant Fastnaught, shifting his black eyes away from my nose for the first time. Fastnaught shrugged and Demeter resumed his inspection; this time he focused on the knot in my tie. "They're going to try to buy it back, huh?"

"That's right."

"And you're the money man?"

"I just carry it."

"How come you?"

I got up from my chair and started toward the door. "Forget it," I said.

"Just hold on, St. Ives," Demeter said. "Don't be so goddamned sensitive."

I turned at the door. "You knew who I was when I walked in the door. The Wingo woman told you about me yesterday or the day before. But you've got to go through your act. The sergeant over there even makes like he's calling Frances Wingo. The only thing wrong with that is her prefix begins with 23 and he dialed 67 or 78 or something. What did he call, the weather or the time?"

Sergeant Fastnaught grinned at me. "The weather.

41

It's a hundred and two outside."

"I know," I said.

"All right, St. Ives," Demeter said. "You can jump down off of your high horse now. You want us to apologize? I'm sorry and Sergeant Fastnaught is sorry, aren't you, Fastnaught?"

"Extremely," Fastnaught said.

"It's just that we don't get many big-time go-betweens from New York," Demeter said, "and we sort of like to see how they tick. In fact, I don't think we ever had a big-time go-between from New York in here before, have we, Fastnaught?"

"Never before," Fastnaught said. "Not from New York. Or from any place else for that matter."

"So, Mr. St. Ives," Demeter said, folding his arms across his chest, "what can we do to make your stay in Washington as pleasant as possible?" His voice dropped from a mellow baritone to a harsh bass. "What're you getting, your usual ten percent?"

"That's right."

"That would be twenty-five thousand," Demeter said.

"Less expenses," I said. "I pay my own."

"Twenty-five thousand," Demeter said, a little dreamily this time. "Fastnaught and I together hardly make that much in a whole year."

"And on top of that you have to buy your own bullets," I said.

Demeter unfolded his arms and leaned across his gray metal desk toward me. "Today I called a guy I know in New York about you," he said. "You know what he told me?"

"No, but something sweet, I hope. You mind if I smoke?"

"Go ahead. Light up. Just be sure you throw the ashes and the butt on the floor. You got to remember this is a police station. This guy in New York I talked to. He said that you're okay in the go-between trade as

42

long as everybody acts like a gentleman. You know. Nice. He said he didn't know how you'd be if things got, well, you know, a little crude. He said you'd never run into one like that."

"That's right," I said. "I haven't."

"That's what my friend in New York said. He also said that you're cautious."

"I thought he said careful," Fastnaught said.

"Fastnaught here was listening in," Demeter said. "Maybe he did say careful, but I thought he said cautious."

"I'm both," I said.

"My friend said you handle these go-between deals just like you play poker. Cautious."

"Careful," Fastnaught said.

"What else did Ogden have to say?" I asked.

"Nothing much; just to tell you hello."

"You going to handle this one in a carefully cautious manner?" Fastnaught said.

"That's right."

"Uh-huh," Demeter said, nodding his big head in a satisfied manner. "Fastnaught and I were hoping you would because whoever stole that shield, what's it called, the shield of—"

"Komporeen," Fastnaught said.

"Yeah, that's right. Komporeen. Sounds like something you'd see about midnight with Maureen O'Sullivan, doesn't it? Well, anyway, Mr. St. Ives, whoever stole the shield of Komporeen might turn out to be just a little crude. You've heard about the dead spade, haven't you?"

"You mean Sackett the guard?"

Demeter nodded. "John Sackett, age 32, Negro, five-feet-eleven, 178 pounds, no visible scars, 430 5th Street, Southeast. Wife, Marthal, and three children. No record. Discovered just off Beach Drive in Rock Creek Park at 10:30 A.M. today by William Ferkiss, eight, and Claude Dextrine, who claimed to be almost

43

nine but was really eight and a half. I didn't see the spade, but Fastnaught here did. Tell him about it, Fastnaught."

The blond sergeant shrugged. "They'd wired his hands behind his back. They'd used a coat hanger to do it. Then they blew the top of his head off with a forty-five. He was a mess, a real mess."

Demeter reached into his desk drawer and took out a cigar in a metal tube. He opened it slowly, licked it with pleasure, and then stuck it in his mouth. After a while he lighted it with a wooden match and blew some smoke up toward the ceiling. "I smoke three of these a day," he said. "I can't afford them really, but I think everybody's entitled to at least one vice. Take Fastnaught here. He's not married so he could afford good cigars but he doesn't even smoke. But he's got a vice. You know what he does? He indulges himself in women, girls really. Real young ones. But like I said, everybody's entitled to at least one vice. What's yours, St. Ives?"

"Punchboards," I said.

"You mean those things where you stick a little metal key in and then get a piece of paper that tells you if you won anything or not?"

"That's right; punchboards."

"They're illegal here," Fastnaught said.

"In New York, too, but I've got my own private supply."

"You're bullshitting me," Fastnaught said.

I smiled at him pleasantly and Demeter took his cigar out of his mouth and waved it around as if he wanted the floor. "Now wait a minute, Fastnaught... isn't that a hell of a name? Fastnaught." He chuckled a little in appreciation. Fastnaught rose and went over to the window and peeked out through the venetian blind; maybe they had a view of the Capitol after all.

"Like I said," Demeter went on, "everybody's entitled to at least one vice. Now I've got cigars and Fastnaught's got his little girls and St. Ives says he's queer for punchboards. There's nothing wrong with that. But what do you think the spade's vice was?"

"You know what it was," Fastnaught said, still peering out through the slats of the venetian blind.

"Yes, I know, but St. Ives here, he doesn't know."

Fastnaught turned and stared at me. "Punchboards," he said. Then suddenly he smiled and went back to the chair behind his desk. "Sackett had a habit. A hundred- to a hundred-and-fifty-dollar-a-day habit and it was getting bigger. That's what his wife said. And he fed it, that's the funny thing. He didn't go out boosting department stores on Thursday night; he didn't stick up any Safeways or gas stations. He just got up about noon and went down to work at four with his needle and his sweet grape soda and his candy bars in his lunch bucket. Now the Coulter Museum pays its guards about six bills a month so where do you think Sackett got the money to feed his habit?"

"How long had he been hooked?" I said.

Demeter waved his cigar around. "Two months; maybe a little more."

"What's his wife say?"

Demeter looked at his watch. "Well, at about eleven o'clock this morning she was telling Fastnaught here that she didn't care whether the son of a bitch was dead or not because he'd gone off to work Friday and left her without a speck of heroin in the house. She ought to be screaming her head off by now because we got her locked away and she's got a habit just about as big as her husband's. Now just where do you think they managed to get two or three hundred dollars a day to keep the nasties away?"

"It's not hard to guess," I said.

"No," Demeter said, "it isn't, is it?"

It was quiet in the small green office for a while. Sergeant Fastnaught took out a stick of gum, unwrapped it slowly, folded it into thirds, popped it into his mouth, and chewed rhythmically while he studied the well-polished toes of his black shoes that he had propped up on one corner of his gray desk. Lieutenant Demeter swiveled his chair so that he had a view of the drawn venetian blind. I admired the back of his neck and the way that his hair curled in tight little waves over his white collar. Demeter sighed, got out of his chair, and moved the two feet to the window where he peeked out through one of the slats in the blind.

"You want to know how Fastnaught and I figure it?" he said to the blind.

"How?" I said.

"We checked on the guard, Sackett, you know. He worked the four-to-twelve shift at the museum, Tuesday through Saturday. His wife wouldn't or couldn't tell us much. She didn't even know the name of the pusher. The neighbors said that the Sacketts were quiet, sent the oldest kid to the first grade every morning and all. The two youngest aren't old enough to go to school yet. The only thing they noticed, the neighbors, I mean, is that the Sacketts the past few weeks have just got quieter and quieter. They didn't go out, not even on Sundays and Mondays when Sackett was off. You can do that on dope, you know. It's not like booze. You can keep going through the motions of everyday living, wash the dishes, clean the house, go to the job, and all. Everything's fine as long as you got your supply."

"What was that doctor's name?" Fastnaught asked. "The one who was hooked and kept on operating, three, maybe four or five times a day."

"His name was Mager," Demeter said. "Now there's one who really had a habit, but he just kept on carving away and nobody ever suspected anything."

"What happened?" I said.

"He scheduled ten operations for one day, woke up,

and decided he couldn't face it so he turned himself in. Right here. Well, not exactly here, it was down the hall. He's down in Lexington still, I understand."

"He was a hell of a fine doctor," Fastnaught said.

"Uh-huh," Demeter said. "Well, we checked out the guys that Sackett worked with at the museum and they hadn't noticed anything different. Sackett had always kept to himself kind of and he just got to be more of a loner, they said. He did his work all right, but that just meant punching in every twelve minutes while he covered his area."

"He was assigned to the African Exhibition?" I said.

"Right," Demeter said. "It's a pretty big exhibit. You get a chance to look at it?"

"No," I said.

"You ought to drop by. They got some real interesting stuff although it's a little weird in my opinion."

"I liked the masks," Fastnaught said. "They got some of the goddamndest masks you ever saw. Real Halloween stuff."

"Well," Demeter said, "Sackett asked to be assigned to the African exhibit. It wasn't anything unusual. They change the guards around all the time. Some come off the day shift and go on nights. Some trade off from the midnight-to-eight shift with those who work the four-to-midnight. The museum closes at six and then the guard complement is reduced by forty percent. Sackett was assigned to the African exhibit because he was the first to apply for it. Fact is, he applied for it a month before it opened."

"He'd been hooked by then?" I said.

"Probably," Demeter said. "The way I figure it is that the bunch who stole this shield knew they couldn't get into that place without inside help. It's wired with the goddamndest alarm system you ever saw. Electric eyes all over the place. Pressure plates. You name it. So they picked Sackett, promised him a fat share, got him hooked on heroin, even got him to

47

get his wife hooked, kept him well supplied, and the day after the exhibit opened they waltzed off with the prize piece."

"How'd they get in," I said, "through the front door?"

"I don't think they ever got in," Demeter said, and puffed some cigar smoke at the ceiling and cocked an eye at me to see how I liked his last statement.

"Why not?"

"The doors," Fastnaught said. "They're electrically sealed at six o'clock."

"Except one," Demeter said.

"That's right," Fastnaught said. "Except one."

"It's an emergency door that leads from the basement up a ramp to the loading area in the rear. It's electrically sealed only one way. What I mean is that the door can be opened from the inside without touching off the alarm system, but it can't be opened from the outside without all hell breaking loose. You follow me?"

I said that I did.

"The guards use the door to change shifts and it's also got something to do with fire-department regulations. I figure that since Sackett had twelve-minute check-in intervals he could use one of them to carry the shield down to the ramp that led to the emergency door. A couple of punch-in intervals later he could carry it up the ramp, open the door, hand it to the thieves, and then make it back upstairs in time to punch in again. He'd give his buddies a half hour or so to get clear and then report the shield as stolen."

"Did he report it?" I said.

"He reported it."

"And there was no full-time guard on that emergency door?"

"No."

"Did you talk to him? Sackett, I mean."

"Me and Fastnaught were off. I was home in bed

48

when it happened; God knows whose bed Fastnaught was in."

Fastnaught chewed his gum a little more rapidly, making it pop on every third or fourth chew. "She'd just turned eighteen," he said. "In fact, it was her birthday. I gave her a real nice present."

"You don't have to lie to us," Demeter said mildly.

"When were you assigned to the thing?" I said.

"Friday," Demeter said. "When we came on our shift. We went looking for Sackett, but by then he'd disappeared. You know something, St. Ives?"

"What?"

"About all we've got on this is the Sackett woman."

"Shit, she doesn't know anything," Fastnaught said.

"Well, I might go along with that, but maybe she does and maybe she doesn't. But I didn't say she was the only thing we've got. I said she was *about* the only thing."

"What else is there?" Fastnaught said.

"Why, we've got ourselves a fancy New York-type go-between, Sergeant Fastnaught, that's what we've got."

Fastnaught took his feet from the desk and put them back on the floor. He leaned forward, his jaws moving rapidly on his stick of gum, and stared at me with his blue eyes. I noticed that they seemed a little bloodshot. "That's right," he said, "we have Mr. St. Ives."

"Who's going to be most cooperative," Demeter said, and smiled at me in a happy, friendly way as if I'd just told him that the promotion had gone through after all and he would be Captain Demeter come next Wednesday morning.

I decided it was time to go. I got up and moved toward the door. "Thanks very much for the information, gentlemen. If you break the case before eight-thirty this evening, I'll be at the Madison. After that, I'll be in New York."

"Did you hear that, Sergeant Fastnaught? Mr. St.

Ives will be at the Madison until eight-thirty."

"I figured the Madison," Fastnaught said. "The Hilton's getting too commercial."

"If you hear of anything from the people—probably just some irresponsible kids who thought it'd be a good joke—anyway if you hear anything from the people who stole the shield of Komporeen, you'll let us know, won't you?" Demeter said, waving his cigar again. "Through no fault of your own, you're sort of mixed up in a murder now, Mr. St. Ives, and we'd more or less like you to stay in touch, if it's not too much trouble."

"No trouble at all," I said. "I always like to support my local police."

"Well, that's good to hear because I'm sure we'll be seeing a lot of each other," Demeter said. "Just one more thing."

"What?" I said.

"You be careful," he said, and then grinned at me around his cigar as if he had just told a very funny and extremely dirty joke.

"And cautious, too," Fastnaught called as I closed the door behind me and went down the green and black marble hall, into the bronze-doored elevator, and out into the yellow sunlight. I walked around until I spotted the window with the lowered venetian blind, and when I found it I was pleased to note that the only view it had was that of a parking lot.

5

I was surprised that it was a woman's voice. She called a little before six, just after I had finished a second bottle of beer and an editorial in *The Washington Star* that took an extremely dim view of a Russian reply to a State Department note protesting the treatment of a couple of American tourists in Moscow. Not only didn't *The Star* much care for the tone of the Russian note, but it also seemed to feel that the two tourists would have done far better to have spent their vacations at Grand Canyon or Rehoboth Beach.

"Would you please listen carefully to what I say, Mr. St. Ives?" the woman said, and it sounded as if she were reading the words and wasn't at all used to it.

"I'm listening," I said.

"You will fly back to New York tomorrow morning and stay in your room at the Adelphi Hotel until six o'clock in the evening. If you have not received a phone call by then, you can leave. If you are not called on Tuesday, then on Wednesday, at 11 o'clock in the morning, you will go to the first phone booth on the left in the lobby of the Eubanks Hotel on East 33rd. At exactly 11 o'clock you will be called. Do you want me to repeat it?"

"No," I said. "I understand."

There were no good-bys and when she hung up I went back to my chair and newspaper and beer, but I could no longer get interested in the danger of air pollution and the beer seemed flat. I tried to remember how many calls there had been during the last four years from nervous men in phone booths who had something that they wanted me to buy back for the persons from whom they had stolen it. Sometimes they whispered, sometimes they talked through their handkerchiefs, and a few had even attempted foreign accents. Each of them had his own complicated set of instructions, sometimes so complicated that they probably bordered on paranoia. Each of the schemes had begun as somebody's daydream and each was wrapped in a curious childlike quality of "let's pretend." But if they seemed the product of a child's fantasy, they invariably were enveloped in the unemotional and unpredictable cruelty that children often have.

My trade had one compensation, however, and I took it out of my wallet and admired it briefly. Then, tired of playing at Silas Marner, I put the check back, walked over to the phone, and dialed a number. When it stopped ringing I asked for Lieutenant Demeter. He came on briskly, barking "Robbery Squad, Lieutenant Demeter," loudly enough for the phone to crackle.

"This is St. Ives. They just called. It was a woman."

"Go on," he said.

"They want me to go back to New York and wait for them to call. If they don't call me at my place tomorrow, they'll call me at a booth in a hotel on Wednesday."

"How did she sound?"

"Like she was reading it."

"She say anything about money?"

"No."

Demeter sighed. "Okay," he said, "I'll get you some company tomorrow."

"Who?"

"They'll be wearing badges with New York Police Department on them. Or the FBI if you want. It looks like it's interstate now."

"No," I said.

"What do you mean no?"

"Just what it usually means. I've been hired to buy back the shield. If I start moving around with cops or FBI agents in tow, there won't be any buy. When I get the shield back you can have everything I've learned and everything I've guessed and between now and then I'll keep you filled in, but until I get the shield back I work alone. If that doesn't fit in with your plans, the museum will have to find another go-between."

"That's probably a damned good idea," Demeter said. "I'd be all for it if the other side would, although I hear that they won't, so it looks like we're stuck with you."

"Get unstuck," I said.

"What'd you say?"

"I said make up your mind."

He was silent for a moment. "All right, St. Ives, we'll go along. But if you're interested in what I think, which you're probably not, I think you're making a mistake. The reason I think you're making a mistake is because whoever you're dealing with have already killed one guy. They could round it out to a couple and they'd still be way ahead after they got the money."

"But not until after they got it," I said.

"I hope you're as bright as you think you are. I hope you're even half as bright."

"Not bright, careful."

"Careful," he said. "I almost forgot about that."

53

"Anything else?"

"Just one item."

"What?"

"The spade's wife."

"What about her?"

"She won't be giving us any more information about Sackett."

"Why?"

"She hung herself about an hour ago," Demeter said, and banged his phone down in my ear.

I had just finished a steak that wasn't quite as good as the menu had promised it would be and was waiting for the elevator when he appeared at my elbow wearing a mauve coat of Edwardian cut with eight brass buttons down its front, a cream-colored shirt whose six-inch-long points were filled by a scarlet neckpiece with a knot the size of a small piece of pie, and a smile so dazzling that it could have lighted up a fairly dim room.

"Mr. St. Ives, I believe," he said, bowing formally from the waist. There was a lot to bow: he was about two inches shorter than the elevator doors and not quite as wide. As he bowed I had the chance to admire his fawn trousers with their burnt orange windowpanes and the brushed green suede shoes that were topped by a pair of large silver buckles.

"I'm St. Ives," I said.

"Permit me," he said, and whisked out a small leather case from which he extracted an ivory card and handed it to me. It was engraved in a swirly italic script which read: Conception Mbwato.

Not only was Mr. Mbwato a very big man, he was also a very black man with skin the color and sheen of ripe eggplant. His accent was good BBC British and he didn't offer to shake hands.

"How can I help you, Mr. Mbwato?" I said, looking up into his unlined face with its broad flat nose, wide, thick mouth, and curiously gentle eyes. Or perhaps they were just sad.

"I thought we might have a little chat," he said.

"About what?"

"The shield of Komporeen."

I nodded. "All right. Where would you like to talk? Here, my room, or in the bar?"

"I think your room would be by far the more preferable."

"All right," I said, "my room."

When we got there, I made a motion toward the largest chair, which Mbwato lowered himself into with a sigh. "It was frightfully hot today," he said. "Even for me."

"You're used to it?" I said.

Mbwato lit up the room again with his smile. "Indeed, Mr. St. Ives, I am used to it."

I was sitting on the chair that went with the writing desk that held the phone. Mbwato crossed his legs and looked around the room as if he thought he might buy it. I lit a cigarette and watched him look. The silence was complete, almost final, as if neither of us would ever speak again, but somehow it was not uncomfortable.

"I am from Brefu," Mbwato said as if that cleared up everything.

"In Jandola," I said.

Mbwato shook his head. "Not in Jandola, Mr. St. Ives," he said gently. "In Komporeen."

"You've been having some trouble there."

"A great deal of trouble, and I am afraid that it will grow much worse before it grows better."

"I'm sorry to hear that," I said.

"Are you really? Why?"

"There's nothing to be said in defense of human suffering," I said. "From what I've read, there's a great deal of it going on in your country."

"More than most persons realize, far more. But I'm

not here to talk about my country except in a rather tangential manner. I'm here to talk about the shield of Komporeen, which you have been engaged to buy back from the thieves who stole it from the Coulter Museum."

"You seem sure about that."

"Quite. And you can rest assured, Mr. St. Ives, that none of the persons with whom you have been dealing has betrayed the confidential nature of either your proposed negotiations or the theft itself. It is simply that we have our source within the Jandolaean Embassy, which, of course, has been kept apprised of the entire affair."

"I see."

Mbwato leaned forward in his chair and rested his elbows on his knees. Even seated he seemed to loom over me. "Do you know much about the shield of Komporeen, Mr. St. Ives, other than that you have been authorized to offer $250,000 for its return?"

"Not really," I said. "I know it's about a yard in diameter, that it weighs sixty-eight pounds, that it is regarded as something of a symbol, a vital one, I suppose, by both your people and those whom you're fighting, and that one man has been killed because of it."

"One man in the United States," Mbwato said, "and more than a million in my country. I'm afraid that it has a most bloody history. If we were able to trace that history back for centuries to its origin, the death toll might even reach high into the millions. You seem to understand that the shield of Komporeen is the symbol of authority in my country. It can be compared, but not very closely, with the Crown of England. Or nearer to home and perhaps from a more sentimental viewpoint, at least, it occupies much the same place in the hearts of my countrymen as your original Declaration of Independence does in yours. But even that is not a proper comparison because the shield is more than an historical document. It is the physical embodiment of a legend that exists amongst a people who give very high credence to their legends. But not only do the Komporeeneans value it, so also do the Jandolaeans, and many, many terrible wars have been fought for its possession. In sum, if one were to combine the sentimental, symbolic, and emotional values of the Crown of England, the Cross of Christianity, and your own Declaration of Independence, then one would have some inkling of how the shield is regarded by my people. And, I suppose," he added thoughtfully, "by the Jandolaeans."

Mbwato stopped talking and the silence crept back into the room. He sat there, dwarfing his chair, staring at the carpet. Then he began to talk or rumble again. His voice went with his size, a deep bass that seemed to escape from far down in his chest.

"The war for us has been going badly," he said, still gazing at the carpet. "We are short of everything, of ammunition, of weapons, of petrol, and of food. Especially food. The government of Komporeen (and I assure you, Mr. St. Ives, we *do* have a government) has been recognized by only a handful of countries, mostly African, and almost as poor as we. But there is a good chance, an excellent chance, I should say, that two major European powers will soon grant us recognition and along with it, much-needed aid in the form of food and weaponry."

"What countries?" I said.

"Strangely enough, France and Germany."

"That is strange."

"Yes, I agree. Britain, of course, is siding with Jandola and your own country has adopted what some have referred to as a 'hands-off' policy. In effect, this means that they're following Britain's lead. As for Russia—well, Russia is supplying both sides, clandestinely to us, openly to Jandola."

"I didn't know that."

"You do not believe it?" he said, and stared at me in a reproachful manner.

"I didn't say I didn't believe it; I said I didn't know it."

"I'm sorry," Mbwato said. "I believe I'm becoming hypersensitive. It's something I'll have to watch. But to continue, Mr. St. Ives, the support from and recognition by France and Germany seems to hinge on our ability to continue our battle for independence. If we can hold out another month, two at the most, then we are confident that the recognition—and the aid—will be granted forthwith. *If* we can hold out."

"Don't you think you can?"

Mbwato shook his head. "There is food enough for another month, perhaps even two. Some will starve, of course, but starvation is no stranger to most Africans. There is enough ammunition to continue our fight for perhaps five weeks. With care we can make it last for six. We have the wherewithal to last, Mr. St. Ives. The question is: do we have the will?"

"Do you?"

"Our morale is not what it should be. The war has been going on for nine months now and there have been many casualties. Unlike the Jandolaeans, we Komporeeneans are a cheerful people, a gentle people, more concerned with the art of living than with the art of war. The Jandolaeans are, in fact, envious of us because we are what you call in this country 'quick studies.' We have taken to technology like a crocodile to the river."

"Or a duck to water," I said.

"I was going to say that, but I thought I should employ a cliché that smacked of my own country." He turned on his five-hundred-watt smile again.

"To continue," Mbwato said, "we have the highest literacy rate in West Africa. We repair our own lorries; do our own engineering; manufacture our own bicycles; build our own radio stations and keep them operating along with our power plants. We have been able to do all this and more, much more, because we

58

place an extremely high value on learning and we are, I suppose, the most inquisitive people in all of Africa. We seem always to be asking why."

"It sounds as though you have a good thing going," I said.

"We do—or did," Mbwato said, "but the demands of the Jandolaeans became impossible. We had no choice but to secede and go our own way. I think we shall succeed, providing, of course, that the morale of the people does not disintegrate. And that's why I'm in the United States and that's why I'm having this chat with you."

"It's something to do with the shield, isn't it?"

"Yes, Mr. St. Ives, it is."

"What?"

"To be perfectly and, I suppose, brutally frank with you, we had planned to steal the shield from the museum ourselves. One of our chaps here is a quite brilliant electrical engineer and he had even figured out a way to circumvent that formidable warning system which the museum employs. It was an absolutely brilliant scheme. You see, the shield's return to Komporeen would serve as a tremendous boost to morale. It would give our people the will to continue our fight, not just for two or three months, but for as long as is needed. This must be difficult for a European, or rather an American, to understand, but I can assure you it's quite true."

"I believe you," I said. "When were you planning to steal the shield?"

"Yesterday," Mbwato said. "Sunday."

"But it already had been stolen."

"Yes. We found out about it as soon as our source at the Jandolaean Embassy could get to a safe telephone."

"Well, if somebody had to steal it, I'm sorry it wasn't you. It sounds as though you could use it."

"Thank you, Mr. St. Ives. That's most kind."

"Not at all."

"Now then," he said, "we come to the crux of the matter. We are, as I've told you, most anxious to recover the shield, not only because it would tremendously raise the morale in our country, but because it rightfully belongs to us and not to the Jandolaeans. Our source in the Jandolaean Embassy informs me that you will receive $25,000 to negotiate the return of the shield to the museum. I am authorized and prepared to offer you $50,000 to return it to us. I'm sorry and must apologize that it cannot be more. I assure you that it would be if we could possibly afford it."

When he was through with his proposition he leaned back in his chair and once more turned on his light-of-the-world smile, as if we had just concluded a multimillion-dollar deal that was going to enable both of us to retire to Majorca next week for the rest of our lives.

I smiled back at him and then shook my head slowly. "I'm sorry, Mr. Mbwato, but it's impossible. I can't go back on my commitment to the museum."

He shrugged as if he had expected the answer, gave me another smile, and rose. "I was afraid that you would say that, Mr. St. Ives, but I had to try. I think you understand."

"I think so."

He moved toward the door, a brilliantly dressed black giant, with a winning smile and a losing country. He turned at the door and gave me the warm benefit of that smile again, but his eyes seemed sad and troubled. "You have been most gracious, Mr. St. Ives, and I want to thank you for your courtesy. And perhaps I can thank you best by warning you."

"About what?" I said.

"When I was reciting the many virtues of us Komporeeneans, I neglected to mention one that is well known throughout West Africa, especially by the Jandolaeans."

"What's that?"

"We are among the most cunning thieves in the world. We will try to steal the shield from the thieves who stole it from the museum. Failing that, we shall surely steal it from you. Good night, Mr. St. Ives."

6

Someday, I fear, I shall live in a house in the suburbs with crab grass that I can mow, snow that I can shovel, tax assessments that I can rail against, and a next-door neighbor's wife who will jump into bed of an afternoon, forty-five minutes before she has to pick up the kids at school. But all of this, like my death, is some time off, and though I view both events with equal trepidation, I meanwhile shall continue to live in the disintegrating inner core of the city and make the most of the privacy it affords, the services that it offers, and the rude wit that can be enjoyed while trying to cross almost any street against the red light. "Whassamattah, shithead, colah-blind or sumpthin?" Stimulating.

For nearly three years home had been the Adelphi, a medium-sized, medium-priced residential hotel that catered exclusively to anyone who could scrape up the monthly rent. I had what was known as a de luxe suite, which meant that they had installed a Pullman kitchen sometime in the 1950's and the rent had been increased by fifty percent. In addition to daily maid service, the Adelphi offered a restaurant and bar that were steadfastly ignored by all the printed guides to New York, a cigar stand that was always running out of stamps, and a switchboard answering service that got the messages right at least a third of the time. Two aging bellhops, one during the day and the other from four till midnight, ran a small book along with whatever errands the guests might have in mind.

After the shuttle from Washington finally quit circling LaGuardia and the pilot brought the plane in only forty-five minutes late, I took a cab to the Adelphi. The phone rang while I was unpacking and when I answered it, Myron Greene wanted to know what had happened.

"I got the job," I said.

"That's not what I meant."

"They paid me half in advance."

"Go on."

"The Washington cops figure that it was an inside job and the inside man's already been killed. His wife hung herself. They were both heroin addicts. Or so the Washington cops say."

"Jesus!" Myron Greene said.

"It gets better," I said. "You'll like the next part."

"Just tell what happened."

"Well, I got a call from a woman who said she's representing the thieves. Somebody's supposed to call me here in New York either today or tomorrow. Then there was Conception Mbwato, a representative of Komporeen, which, he says, is the rightful owner of the shield. He offered me fifty thousand to hand the shield over to him, once I get it back. I turned him down—reluctantly, I might add—and he promised to steal it—either from me or from whoever's got it now. And I asked Frances Wingo to have a drink, but she refused."

"You'd better mail me the check," Myron Greene

63

said, "and I'll have Spivack deposit it for you."

"If they have any stamps," I said.

"Who?"

"The cigar stand."

"You're dissembling again," Myron Greene said. "You always do that when you're nervous."

"I'll take something for it. The cigar stand might have something along with the stamps."

"What do you do now?"

"I wait for the phone to ring."

"What did the Washington police say?"

"That I make too much money."

"Do they think that whoever stole it were professionals?"

"I don't think I even asked," I said. "It seemed obvious that they were. They killed the guard, which means two things to me. One, they're either professionals or gifted amateurs, and two, you didn't ask for enough money."

"It's not too late for that in view of subsequent developments," Myron Greene said. "I can probably work something out."

"Do that."

"What are your plans now?"

"As I said, I wait for the phone to ring. Then I might try to find out if anybody knows anything. The thieves know who I am. That means that they might know somebody whom I know. And since they're the types who go around shooting people in the back of the head, perhaps I should find out."

Myron Greene wheezed for a moment. "It might not be a bad idea," he said finally. "As long as it doesn't disrupt the negotiations."

"If I find out that they're the kind who don't leave any witnesses around at all, there won't be any negotiations."

"You have to remember that you've already committed yourself."

"Not to get killed," I said.

"Of course not. I didn't mean that."

"You mean you need $2,500?"

"No, damn it, I don't need $2,500 and if you think my fee is too high, I'll forget about it."

"Calm down, Myron. Remember what excitement does to your asthma."

"Screw my asthma, St. Ives." Myron Greene never called me St. Ives unless he was upset.

"What's bothering you?" I said.

"I received a call this morning from Washington."

"From Frances Wingo?"

"No. From the State Department."

"What do they want?"

"They, or rather an assistant under-secretary for African Affairs, a Mr. Littman Cox, wants Jandola to get that shield back. This Mr. Cox—I think he said he was an assistant under-secretary, whatever that is— wanted to know if the State Department could be of any assistance."

"How?" I said.

"That's what I asked him. He said that he could bring in the FBI."

"What did you tell him, Myron?" I said.

"Don't get that tone in your voice, St. Ives," he said. "I told him that it would be totally unnecessary and that we preferred to work alone and that if he wanted to be of assistance to us, he could make sure that the FBI stayed out of the case until the transaction was completed."

I decided that Myron Greene liked having the State Department call him. Even more, he liked turning them down and getting himself into what he considered to be the thick of things and referring to us and we. "What else did the assistant under-secretary of State for African Affairs have to say after you said no?"

"Well, to be frank, he seemed upset. He kept telling me that I was in no position to assess the international significance of the shield and that its return was of what he called—I even wrote it down here—'paramount salience to the future relations between Jandola and the United States.' He sounded like a prick."

"All that means is that State is cozying up to the British and doesn't want either France or Germany to start giving aid to Komporeen."

"How do you know that?" Myron Greene said.

"Conception Mbwato told me."

"I see," Myron Greene said, and from the tone of his voice I could tell that he didn't see at all, but the story was too long to tell. "Anyway," he said, "I turned him down and told him that if he brought the FBI in, we would back out."

"What did he say when you said that?"

"He wanted to know about your professional competence and integrity."

"You assured him that they are of the highest order, of course."

"Of course. I also pressed him about the use of the FBI; he promised me that they would not be called in. You know something?"

"What?"

"Perhaps I should have gone into the diplomatic service instead of law—especially if Cox is typical of what State has working for it."

"You could have made a great contribution," I said with as much sincerity as I could muster.

"I might've at that," Myron Greene said. "Keep me informed, Philip."

"Every step of the way."

When he hung up I called down to the desk and asked Eddie, the day bellhop, to bring me up a steak sandwich and a glass of milk.

"Steak's not too good today," he said.

"How's the liverwurst?"

"Better."

"Make it a liverwurst."

While I waited for him, I endorsed the check, put it in an envelope, and addressed it to Myron Greene. When Eddie arrived with the sandwich, I paid him, gave him two dollars to put on a horse I'd picked on the plane, and a letter to mail.

"They're out of six-cent stamps at the cigar stand again," he said. "But I got some."

"How much?"

"Dime each?"

"I'll buy one," I said, and handed him a dime. It's what I've always liked about New York. Neighborly.

I ate the sandwich and spent the rest of the afternoon waiting for the phone to ring and reading a paperback novel that I'd picked up in the Washington airport. It was about a CIA man who wandered around Red China for a couple of years doing good works like poisoning the water supply.

By six o'clock the phone hadn't rung so I waited until six-fifteen and then dialed a number. A man's voice said, "A to Z Garage."

"Parisi there?"

"Who?"

"Parisi," I said slowly, pronouncing each syllable with care. "Johnny Parisi."

"Nobody here by that name."

"Just tell him it's Philip St. Ives."

"St. what?"

"Ives," I said. "You want me to spell it?"

"Lemme see."

I waited a while and then Parisi came on the phone with, "Hello, Lucky."

"I like your new secretary."

"You mean Joey. He's something, isn't he?"

"Something's as good a description as any."

"By the way, when I got home last Saturday from your place, I found out I really took a bath. I dropped nearly nine hundred bucks and most of it to Ogden."

"He needs it. His daughter's starting to college next month."

"Like shit he needs it. With what he knocks down he could send a dozen of them to college and never miss it."

67

"Nobody's that rich."

"Maybe you're right," Parisi said. "It ain't like when you and me were going to college. I don't understand these kids today, always raising hell and trying to take over the schools."

"They're different," I said.

"Maybe they ought to have to work their way through like we did," Parisi said, apparently convinced that missing six set shots in a row qualified as work.

"You free for dinner tonight?" I said.

"I've got to see a guy downtown about ten."

"Come over around eight and I'll buy you a steak."

"Dominic's?" he said.

I sighed. Dominic's meant a forty-dollar tab at least. "Dominic's."

"Okay," Parisi said. "At eight." I started to say goodby, but he said, "You're working again, aren't you?"

"I'm working."

"I figured as much," he said, and hung up.

Dominic's was a medium-sized restaurant on West 54th Street that had leaped into popularity and a measure of notoriety after a Hollywood motion-picture star began to use it as his New York headquarters because it was quiet, the food was good, and a friend of his who was fairly prominent in the criminal hierarchy owned thirty percent of it. The actor once held court in a small alcove just off the main dining room until the word got around and the out-of-town tourists started to flock there and order things like spaghetti and meatballs and even pizza, which made the chef angry enough to threaten to quit. The movie star stopped coming, the owners raised the prices, and the out-of-towners flocked to other places where they could goggle at some celebrity who was worth talking about when they got back home to Joplin or Cedar Falls. Or to Chicago and Dallas for that matter. The citizens of Joplin and Cedar Falls are not the nation's only celebrity gogglers.

Now Dominic's was once more quiet, the food was excellent, the prices remained astronomic, the chef was happy, and the restaurant fulfilled its original purpose of losing money for its owners, whose accountants employed the deficit to offset the profits from other businesses which were not quite so respectable.

Parisi was already there, chewing on a piece of celery, when I arrived a few minutes after eight. He waved the stalk around as he chomped on the vegetable. "I'm trying to quit smoking," he said. "They say that celery helps."

"Good luck," I said, and lighted a cigarette.

"Oh, hell," Parisi said, and fished out his amber cigarette holder. "Let me borrow one from you; I'll quit tomorrow."

We ordered drinks, a martini each, and then began to study the menu.

"You hungry?" Parisi asked.

"Fairly so."

"Me, too. I didn't have any lunch. You want to go a chateaubriand?" A chateaubriand was $27.50.

"Fine."

Parisi grinned at me around his cigarette holder. "Like I said, I'm hungry."

Parisi got into a long conversation in Italian with the waiter about how the steak should be cooked, the salad prepared, and what wine to order. I looked around the restaurant, which was only half full. The alcove where the actor formerly held court was dark and empty and I felt that perhaps it should be turned into a national shrine. While waiting for the steak, Parisi and I talked about poker and drank to absent friends.

"That guy Wisdom took a bath last Saturday, too," Parisi said as he lit another borrowed cigarette.

"He can afford it."

"How much did his grandma leave him, five million?"

"Seven, but it's in a trust fund and he has to live off the income."

"How much do you think that is?"

"At five percent it would be $350,000 a year, but he's probably doing better than that."

"Christ, with that much money he could sure dress a little better than he does." Parisi liked people to be neat.

"With all that money he can afford to be a slob," I said.

Parisi nodded, not so much in agreement, but as if expressing the universal conviction that if he had that much money, he could spend it far more efficiently than could Park Tyler Wisdom III, who went around in sneakers and a sweatshirt, for God's sake.

"What does he do?" Parisi said. "I mean he just doesn't play poker all day long."

"Jokes," I said.

"Jokes? Like in the *Reader's Digest?*"

"No, not like that. Wisdom likes to play elaborate jokes on fairly prominent people who don't have a very good sense of humor."

"Then they don't get the joke."

"That's what makes it funny to Wisdom."

Parisi was interested. "What kind of jokes? I mean do you remember any of them?"

"Well, there's the Bonford Gentry Park story."

"What's that?"

"Wisdom has this farm or estate, I suppose you would call it, in Connecticut. He also had an old Airedale that was half blind who stayed on the estate with the caretaker. The dog must have been thirteen or fourteen years old and it drooled a lot. One time the caretaker took the dog into this small town which is near the estate and it got out of the car and wandered away. It was in the summer and the dog's tongue was hanging out and it was slobbering like old dogs do, especially Airedales. Well, the mayor of the town happened to see it, called the local cops, and they shot it."

"They thought it was a mad dog, huh?" Parisi said.

"That's what they said."

"So what happened?"

"The caretaker got the dog's body and took it back to the estate and buried it. Then he called Wisdom and told him what had happened. Wisdom didn't do anything for a couple of weeks and then he drove up to Connecticut and called on the mayor. There was some property that the city owned which it wanted to turn into a park. Wisdom offered to donate the money for the park improvements provided that they would call it Bonford Gentry Park after an old friend of his. He also offered to put up a fountain. The mayor agreed to all this, even to calling it Bonford Gentry Park. The mayor seemed to think that Wisdom was harmless enough for a millionaire. The park was developed and Wisdom paid for everything—the trees, the swings, the seesaws, the shrubs and what have you. The plumbing for the fountain was installed and the day before the park was to open Wisdom had the fountain trucked in at night, erected behind canvas, and connected to the plumbing.

"The next day was Saturday and the unveiling of the new fountain. After a speech that thanked Wisdom for his contribution to the town, the mayor pulled the cord that unveiled the fountain. The water was turned on at the same time. Around the base of the fountain was the inscription: To Bonford Gentry, Dear Friend and Close Companion, 1954-1968. The fountain was an eight-foot statue of Bonford Gentry, who, of course, was the Airedale that the mayor had ordered shot. His left leg was cocked up in the air and he was peeing the water. Wisdom said it made a pleasant splash."

"Huh," Parisi said. "What did the mayor do?"

"Nothing."

"Didn't he remember the dog and having it shot?"

"No."

"Then he didn't get the point."

"No," I said, "that's what made it so funny to Wisdom."

"Well, it's sure not like those funny stories you read in *Reader's Digest*," Parisi said.

"No, it's not," I said. "It's nothing like those."

When we were through with the chateaubriand, we ordered some $2.00-a-glass brandy and some 75-cent-a-cup coffee. Parisi borrowed another cigarette from me, inserted it into his amber holder, and lit it with one of his own matches.

"Okay," he said around or through the holder, "you didn't buy me a steak just so you could tell me some dog stories."

"You're right."

"What's your problem, one of those go-between deals?"

"Yes."

"Where?"

"Washington," I said. "Do you guys have anything in Washington?"

"Huh uh," Parisi said. "Not a thing. The colored boys have got it all sewed up down there and we just leave them alone. The closest we are to Washington is Baltimore. There's pretty good action in Baltimore."

"I'm supposed to buy something back for $250,000 from whoever stole it. They seemed like pros. They've also killed one guy so I'd like to make sure that they don't have any similar plans for me."

Parisi brushed some imaginary ashes from his double-breasted vest with its flapped pockets. "We got a call about a month and a half ago about you," he said.

"From whom?"

"From a guy who knew a guy who knew a guy who wanted to know something."

"About me?"

"You know, if you were all right and all. I didn't think anything about it. I just told them that we'd never had any business dealings with you, but we knew some people who had and they didn't have any complaints."

"This was how long ago?"

Parisi looked up at the ceiling and started counting on his right hand. "Six weeks at least; maybe seven."

"That could be about right."

"You want to talk to the guy that I talked to?"

"Yes," I said. "I think so."

"He's way down the list, you understand. He may not know a goddamned thing except the name of the guy who asked him to call us."

"I understand."

"You can tell him I told you to call if you want to."

"Thanks."

"You want to write it down."

I found a piece of paper and a ballpoint pen. "Okay."

"His name is Al Shippo. Albert M. Shippo in the phone book."

"What's he do?" I said.

Parisi shrugged. "He hangs around."

"I'll call him."

"Mention my name."

"All right," I said, signaling to the waiter for the check. While I paid it, Parisi drummed on the table with the fingers of his left hand.

"You know something?"

"What?"

"The statue of that dog pissing."

"What about it?"

"I was just thinking," he said. "That might be worth driving over to Connecticut this Sunday just to see."

73

7

At eleven o'clock the next morning I was standing in a musty phone booth in the lobby of the Eubanks Hotel, a seedy, almost furtive establishment that catered in an embarrassed kind of way to the old who, thirty years or so before, had believed those insurance-company advertisements which had lied about how they could retire comfortably on $150 a month.

Except for a middle-aged room clerk behind the desk who seemed to be suffering from a vile hangover, the only occupant of the lobby was a thin, bald oldster with milky blue eyes who looked to be in his seventies. He struggled out of the depths of a battered couch that probably was called a davenport when it was new and hobbled carefully over to the booth.

"You going to be in there long, son?" he asked. "I gotta make a call and the other phone's not working. I gotta call my doctor about some medicine for my sciatica. It hit last night right about—"

The phone rang and I picked it up and said hello,

closing the door of the booth as I nodded pleasantly at the old man who was having trouble with his sciatica, or who just wanted somebody to talk to.

"Mr. St. Ives?" It was a man's voice this time, but it seemed fuzzy and blurred, as if he were speaking through a mouthful of wet cotton.

"Yes."

"The old man who just spoke to you has been paid five dollars to hand you an envelope. In the envelope are instructions. If you follow them exactly, you'll get the shield back." There was a click and the phone went dead.

I turned in the booth and looked at the old man, who was grinning at me and nodding happily. It could have been the most fun he had had since the 1933 World's Fair in Chicago. I put the phone on its hook, opened the door, and stepped out of the booth.

"You the fella?" the old man said.

"If you've got an envelope, I am."

"They gave me five bucks just to hold it till you got here."

"Who gave you five bucks?"

"Kids," he said. "A couple of hippies with long hair and beads. I was sitting here last night watching Lucy when they came in and I figured to myself that they were a little far uptown. But they just looked around and saw me, wasn't nobody else, so they come over and say they're going to lay five bucks on me to give an envelope to a gent who'll be in the phone booth at eleven o'clock this morning. So I says, 'Let's see the five bucks,' and they say okay and give me the five and the envelope. I ain't opened it neither. You with the FBI?"

"No."

"CIA maybe?"

I didn't want to disappoint him. "Treasury," I said.

"T-man, huh?" he said, and looked around the lobby to make sure that nobody was listening. The only one who could have been was the room clerk, who sat behind the desk with his head in his hands, wishing that the world would end.

"You got the envelope?" I said.

"What's it worth to you?"

"Another five. I'd make it more, but they're cracking down in Washington."

"New administration, huh?"

"Right."

He reached into the inside pocket of a shapeless gray coat and brought out an envelope. I reached for it, but he moved his hand away. "You said something about five bucks."

"You're right again." I took out my wallet, found a five, and handed it to him. He handed me the envelope.

"I never opened it," he said. "Can't say I didn't think about it, but I never opened it."

"I'll mention that to the chief," I said.

"Aw, shit," the old man said, turned, and hobbled back to his place on the sofa, which was two feet from a television set that crackled happily away with lots of squeals and laughter.

I didn't open the envelope until I was back in my room at the Adelphi. The contents had been typed on drugstore bond with a manual machine, if that was either a comfort or a clue to Lieutenant Demeter and Sergeant Fastnaught. I felt that it wasn't. There were numerous x-outs and the style was strictly Monopoly imperative:

Get $250,000 in used tens and twenties Thursday. Drive to third Howard Johnson motel on Jersey Turnpike. Check in by six. Do not contact police. Wait in motel for instructions.

I decided that they were indeed professionals. Motels were proving popular in the go-between trade. They were useful for either completing the transaction or for observing how well the intermediary obeyed instructions. A familiar pattern, one which I had followed twice before, was to check into the motel with the money, parking my unlocked car at least six or seven doors away from my room. I waited in my room for a predesignated amount of time and then left, leaving the money in the closet, and the door to the room unlocked. I then went to my car, now locked by the thieves, opened it and looked under the seat for whatever it was that I was supposed to buy back. In both recent cases it had been jewelry. I had been instructed to wait in my car for five minutes until the thieves had the opportunity to make sure that the money was really in the suitcase or the satchel or the airline carryall bag in the closet of the motel room. Then I was free to drive off, bearing the jewels back to their rightful owner, and the thieves could head south to spend the money in Miami or San Juan or Biloxi.

The anonymity that surrounds motels, especially the smaller, cheesier ones that do a brisk hot-bed business, makes them eminently suitable for such transactions. A thief can check in two days before he gives the go-between the instructions to make sure that the police aren't occupying the rest of the rooms. The go-between's advantage lies in his ability to get to a phone quickly if he finds that there's nothing under the front seat of his car. And finally, neither the thieves nor the go-between ever confronts each other, which is primarily to the thieves' advantage unless the go-between is as cautious as I am.

I read the typed message three times and then picked up the phone and placed a person-to-person call to Frances Wingo in Washington. It went through quickly enough when I identified myself to her secretary.

"Good morning," she said.

"Good morning," I said. "I have some news."

"Yes?"

"I've just received a message from whoever has the shield. They want the money Thursday. That's tomorrow."

"All right," she said. "Where shall I bring it?"

"You?"

"I believe it to be my responsibility."

"I won't dispute that. I just thought it might be a little heavy for you. They want it in used tens and twenties and that much money weighs around fifty pounds."

"I'm sure I can manage," she said. "Where shall I bring it?"

"To my hotel, the Adelphi." I gave her the address.

"What time?"

"Any time before three," I said. "If you make it before two, we can have lunch."

She ignored the invitation. Perhaps that's the form for widows of four weeks. "Will you recover the shield tomorrow?" she said.

"I don't know. It's possible."

"Is it probable?"

"Again, I don't know. I have no idea whom I'm dealing with. The trip down the Jersey Turnpike may be just a dry run to find out how well I follow instructions. Or they may be in a hurry for the money and want to get rid of the shield. You've got to remember that it's not something that they can carry around in their hip pocket or unload at the corner pawnshop. There's an extremely limited market." I started to tell her about the fifty thousand that I had been offered by Conception Mbwato, but I decided not to because it was all too complicated and there was no point in listening to questions for which I had no answers.

"I'll call Mr. Spencer to arrange for the money," she said.

"When you get through with that, would you also call Lieutenant Demeter and fill him in on what's happened?"

"I didn't think that you wanted to involve the police."

"I'm not involving them; I'm just staying in touch with Demeter because I said that I would."

"All right," she said. "I'll call him."

"What time shall I expect you tomorrow?"

"After two."

"That's what I thought," I said.

When Frances Wingo hung up in my ear, I decided that we probably would never be close friends, but there seemed to be an excellent chance that we might become polite enemies if either of us wanted to go to the bother. I thought—or brooded—about this during the time it took to find a can of tomato soup and run it through the electric opener. I then poured the soup into a pot, added a half can of water, and placed it over one of the two burners that the Pullman kitchen offered. While the soup heated, I looked up a number in the phone book and dialed it. When a man's voice said, "Albert Shippo and Associates," I asked for Mr. Shippo.

"I'm Shippo."

"My name's Philip St. Ives. I'd like to see you."

"What about?"

"Johnny Parisi suggested that I call. He thought you might have something I could use."

"Parisi, huh?"

"Parisi," I said.

"You a wholesaler?"

"No."

"Well, I tell you, I don't do much retail any more, but if Parisi said to call, then I guess it's okay. You wanta come over?"

"This afternoon all right?"

"Anytime," Shippo said. "I'm not doing anything anyway except sitting here trying out a new cure on my athlete's foot."

"I'll be there at two-thirty."

"Two-thirty, three-thirty, it don't matter," he said. "I ain't going nowhere."

A few minutes after I got through talking to Shippo, the soup was heated so I took it off the burner, poured it into a bowl, found a box of crackers and a bottle of beer, and laid my solitary midday meal on the hexagonal table that had been designed to comfortably accommodate six at poker.

Albert Shippo and Associates' office was at East 24th Street on the eighth floor of the George Building, which was as unimpressive as its name. There were two elevators, but only one of them was working under the captaincy of a shabbily dressed old man with a face the color and texture of a worn peach pit and pure white hair that hung down to his shoulders. He jerked the handle when I said "eight," and when the door didn't close, he kicked it with a scuffed cowboy boot. The elevator responded, grudgingly, it seemed, and we creaked upward.

At the second floor, he turned to look at me. "Don't get any ideas, rube. I ain't one of them just because of the long hair."

"I didn't think that you were."

"Some folks get the wrong idea. I rode with Bill, you know. Madison Square Garden, nineteen-ought-nine."

"Bill?"

"Bill Cody, you dumb shit. William Frederick Cody. Buffalo Bill."

"You were in his Wild West show, huh?"

"Damned right I was. We all wore our hair long like this from Bill on down. Now folks think I'm one of them Village punks, but I ain't. I'm part Indian, too. Chickasaw on my mother's side."

"You must have some great memories," I said as the elevator croaked to a stop at the eighth floor.

"They ain't so hot," the old man said.

Eight-two-nine was the number of Albert Shippo

and Associates and it was down the hall, past the skip-tracer, the direct mail firm, the manufacturer's representative, and three empty offices. Albert Shippo and Associates was lettered on the pebbled-glass door and another message on a typed card that was stuck to the glass with Scotch tape read KNOCK BEFORE ENTERING. I knocked and a voice said come in. Inside there was a scarred golden oak desk positioned in front of the single window with a dark green shade. The window needed washing. There were four metal filing cabinets and two chairs. One of the chairs, also golden oak, was in front of the desk. The other one was behind it and contained Albert M. Shippo and, as far as I could tell, all of the associates.

"You the guy who called?" the man behind the desk said.

"Yes."

"Sit down," he said. "I'm Shippo." He was about forty-five with a double chin and a smooth bald head which he drew attention to with a set of mutton-chop sideburns that fanned out over plump cheeks well below the lobes of his ears. Thick black horn-rimmed glasses covered his eyes, which seemed disappointed when they looked at me, but they may have looked at everything like that. He had a small pink mouth below an ordinary pink nose, and the upper lip of the mouth formed what they used to describe as a perfect Cupid's bow. Below his double chins was a white shirt collar that seemed too small and a blue and white striped tie that was too narrow.

I sat down and looked around the office. There was a black telephone on the desk, but no calendar on the wall. In fact, there was nothing to indicate whether Shippo had moved in that morning or six years before.

"Like I said over the phone, I'm a jobber and don't do much retail business any more," he said. "But since Johnny Parisi told you to call—well..." He let the sentence fade away as if it were just too much trouble to complete.

"I don't know if you got my name right," I said. "It's St. Ives. Philip St. Ives."

Shippo nodded. "I got it okay."

"You called Parisi about me six or seven weeks ago."

"I make a lot of calls. Some guy calls me and says, 'Hey, Al, whaddya know about so and so?' and I say, 'I don't know nothing about so and so,' and the guy says, 'Can you find out?' and I say, 'Okay, it'll cost you ten bucks.' Or twenty or thirty or whatever I can hit him up for. So I call around and find out what I can and then I call the guy back and say, 'So and so's okay' or 'So and so's a bum who owes everybody in town.' But that ain't my main business. Like I said, I'm a jobber."

"Of what?" I said.

"High-class art. Say a guy wants to go into business for himself. You know, he's got a full-time job but he wants to get into something he can run out of his home. I put him in business. Direct mail. Let the post office do the hustling, I say." He reached into his desk drawer, took out a sheet of paper, and slid it across the desk to me. "This has been one of my hottest numbers. About a thirty-percent return on this one and that's goddamned high in the direct-mail business."

I picked up the letter-sized sheet of paper and looked at it. It was a Xeroxed copy of a handwritten letter and was addressed to "Hi, Friend!" In the upper right-hand corner was the blurred picture of a nude man and woman. The body of the letter read:

I'm Sally and that's Bill you see there with me. We're a liberal minded young couple and we don't mind showing you the things we enjoy doing together and with our friends. I'm blonde and cute. Bill is tall and very well endowed. I measure 36-24-36.

We went to Mexico City last month with some girl friends of mine and visited one of those little known

82

exotic night spots you hear about for mature minded people. Because of their unusual nature, these places are illegal here and mighty hard to find down there. But I'm sure you've heard about them and all the wild things that go on inside.

We took some photos of each other with another couple that was there. Some of us girls by ourselves and the rest show us couples in almost every position possible. These aren't any of those phony nudist photos. These are the *real* thing.

I'll sell you a whole set in black and white for $8.00 or four sets in color for $12.00. I'll include some very special shots they took of me and Betty together. Send me the money and I'll rush them right back to you.

It was signed, "Sincerely yours, Sally."

I tossed the letter back on the desk. "Business pretty good, huh?" I said.

"Getting better all the time," Shippo said. "I furnish the whole thing: the letter, the photos, and the sucker list. They mail out the letter once they get copies Xeroxed and then sit back and wait for the dough to roll in. They make money, I make money, and a lot of lonely people get their jollies. You want a set of the colored shots? I can let you have them for fifty bucks."

"It said twelve in the letter."

"I might throw in a little information," Shippo said.

"Fifty is still steep."

Shippo leaned back in his chair, which squeaked, placed his fat hands on the bare desk, and smiled at me with yellow teeth that seemed too large and square for his small mouth. "That's a nice suit you got on," he said. "I know suits. I figure you're worth fifty."

"You remember my name, now?"

"St. Ives," he said. "It ain't a name you forget or if you do, you remember it when somebody brings it up. Fifty bucks?"

I nodded. "Fifty bucks."

"Let me get you your pictures first." He moved over to one of the files, took out a nine-by-eleven-inch manila envelope, peeked inside to make sure that it was the right one, and then sat back down in his chair. I took out my wallet, found two twenties and a ten, and pushed them over to him. He handed me the envelope. "You want a receipt?" he said.

"Just information. Such as who asked you to call Parisi about me?"

Shippo took the three bills and folded them lengthwise. Then he folded them in half, then folded them again, and tucked them into his watch pocket. "That was a couple of months back, wasn't it?"

"Was it?"

"Yep, I remember now. It was a couple of months back."

"In June," I said.

"In June."

"Now we have when, let's try who."

Shippo looked around his desk as if he wished that there were some papers to shuffle. There weren't so he opened a drawer and brought out a bottle of Old Cabin Still and two smeared glasses that looked like they had once contained Kraft cheese spread. He poured them half full and then moved one of them over to my side of the desk. "I always have a drink about this time of day," he said. "Doctor says it's good for my blood pressure. I got high blood pressure." He picked up his glass and drained it, sighed, and wiped his mouth with the back of his hand. "Drink up," he said. I picked up the bourbon and took a swallow out of politeness and then put the glass back on the desk. I don't care much for bourbon.

"Funny thing the way your name came up, you know," Shippo said. "Guy I hadn't seen in five, maybe six years calls up and wants to know if I know anybody who might give him a once-over on a Philip St. Ives, so I tell him that I know lots of people and he

84

says, no, not those kind, he needs somebody who's got a good reputation, like his word is his bond, who's respectable and all. So I say how about my good friend Johnny Parisi, is he good enough for you? And the guys says, you know Johnny Parisi? And I tell him that Johnny and me have been friends for a long time."

"What else did he say?"

"Nothing. He just wanted me to call Parisi and find out about you."

"Find out what?"

"Find out if you were okay, A-1, and would do what you said you would do. You wanta know what Johnny said about you?"

"No," I said. "I want to know who asked about me."

"Oh, him. He was only good for thirty bucks, but what the hell, it only took a couple of phone calls."

"All right," I said. "Who?"

"A guy name of Frank Spellacy, but you gotta understand that he was only calling me about you for a friend of his."

"Where can I find Spellacy?" I said.

"In the phone book. Manhattan."

"What's he do?"

"You mean for a living?"

"For a living."

Shippo shrugged. "What does anybody do? Me, I think of myself as an art dealer who provides a service for lonely people and believe me, there're a lot of lonely people around. But you know what those creeps from the post office said I was? They said I was a hard-core pornographer. So I said to hell with them. I don't use the post office no more. I send everything out by messenger if it's close by, and Railway Express if it ain't."

"They must have hated to lose your business," I said.

"You mean the post office?"

"Uh-huh."

"Nah. They got so much business they can't take care of it now."

"You don't have any idea of what Spellacy does?"

"He dabbles in this and that."

"Such as?"

"Well, five or six years ago he was running a securities firm."

"You mean a boiler room."

"You call it a boiler room. Me and Spellacy called it a securities firm. I was helping out in the afternoons and we were doing pretty good until there was a misunderstanding and, well, Spellacy had to liquidate. I didn't hear nothing about him for a couple of years. I think he was out of town."

"He must have drawn a short sentence."

"His lawyer wasn't too hot," Shippo said. "You gotta have a top lawyer if you wanta survive in the business world which, when you come right down to it, ain't nothing but a jungle, like Jimmy Hoffa said. Now there's probably one of the most unappreciated men in the country. And look what they done to him."

"History will justify him," I said. "But let's get back to Spellacy. You don't have any idea of what he's doing?"

"He did mention something about real estate, come to think of it. He said he's got some big development going out in Arizona."

I got up. "Thanks for the information."

Shippo didn't stir, other than to wave his hand. "Glad to oblige."

I was heading for the door when he called me back. "Hey, your pictures."

I went back to the desk and picked up the envelope. "You're right," I said. "It's what I really came for."

On the way to the elevator I looked at the photographs. They were the usual assortment of duets and threesomes and, if I'd had more time, I might have grown interested. When the elevator came with its ancient pilot, I got on and stood at the back.

"You like dirty pictures?" I said.

"Who don't?" the old man said.

"Here," I said, and handed him the envelope.

He accepted the envelope, slipped out the first picture, and cackled. Then he placed them under his stool. "I'll save 'em till I get off," he said. "How come you don't want 'em?"

I tapped myself on the chest. "Bad heart."

The old man turned and grinned at me evilly. Then he ducked down for the envelope, took another peek, and shook his head in admiration. "You're right about one thing, rube."

"What?"

"They're sure as hell dirty."

8

The tall black young man who leaned casually against the front fender of the Chrysler that was illegally parked in front of the George Building wasn't trying to be inconspicuous. Not with a lemon-colored suit and a shirt the shade of a ripe tangerine. When it came to the selection of a tie, he had deserted the citrus family for neckwear that had the luster and sheen of dark purple grapes. The oyster-white raincoat that was draped over his right forearm also helped to set him apart from the rest of the pedestrians, most of them in shirt sleeves. And then, too, it hadn't rained in New York for almost three weeks.

I gave him only a glance as I came out of the building and turned left, headed for a bar or a drugstore and a phone book to look up the number and address of Frank Spellacy. I had taken just five steps when he caught up with me on the left, the raincoat still draped over his right forearm.

"Mr. St. Ives?"

I stopped and turned. "Yes."

"Mr. Mbwato was wondering whether he could give you a lift." He had a voice similar to Mbwato's, though not nearly so deep. It was a nice tenor with all of the African edges smoothed away and if I had closed my eyes, it could have been David Niven asking, ever so politely, whether I could possibly use a ride.

"Not today, thanks," I said, and started to turn away but stopped when the oyster-white raincoat dug into my side with something that could have been a gun or a pen or even an unusually stiff forefinger. I decided that it was a gun.

"Come on," I said. "This is ridiculous."

"Isn't it just?" the tall young man said, and smiled gently. "But you see, I have my instructions and when I don't follow them through to completion, Mr. Mbwato becomes most upset."

"That's a gun under your coat, not just your finger?"

"I'm afraid it's a gun, Mr. St. Ives."

"I could yell. For a cop."

"There is none to hear."

"I could just yell."

He smiled again and looked to be genuinely amused. "What response do you think your fellow New Yorkers would make? A sidelong glance? A derisive smile? Come now, Mr. St. Ives."

"I could run."

"Then I would surely shoot you. Probably in the leg," he added thoughtfully.

"All right," I said. "Where's Mbwato?"

"Just down the street. We had quite some difficulty in finding a place to park."

I turned and the young black man turned with me, his raincoat-covered arm still aimed at my left kidney. "How did you know I was here?"

"In the George Building? We observed you going in; we assumed that you would be coming out."

"You followed me from the hotel then?"

"Yes, Mr. St. Ives, we did."

The car was an appropriately black seven-passenger Cadillac that, according to the license number, had been rented for the occasion. The tall young man opened the rear door for me and I climbed in. Mbwato was seated in the back, making the car look smaller than it was, and another black man was behind the wheel. The one with the raincoat walked around the car and got in beside the driver.

"Mr. St. Ives," Mbwato said in his bass voice which sounded as though it had started somewhere down near the subway. "What a distinct pleasure to see you again. Where can we drop you?"

"My hotel would be nice."

"Of course. Mr. St. Ives' hotel," he said to the driver. Mbwato, really dwarfing the rear of the Cadillac, wore a different suit this time, a dark green one with brass buttons on its vest, a white shirt with a widespread collar and a paisley tie. Everything fitted admirably and for all I knew he may have been patronizing Myron Greene's tailor.

"Why?" I said.

"I beg your pardon."

"Why the gunpoint invitation?"

"Gunpoint?" he said. "There was no gun."

"Your friend in the front seat said there was."

Mbwato chuckled and sounded like an amused bullfrog. "Did Mr. Ulado tell you that he had a gun?"

"He did."

Mr. Ulado turned in his seat and smiled at me. He held up a fountain pen and winked. "This was the gun, Mr. St. Ives. I apologize for my method of persuasion, but Mr. Mbwato did so much wish to have this chat with you."

"It's really my fault," Mbwato said. "I urged Mr. Ulado to make the invitation as convincing as possible. He must have been carried away."

"He did fine," I said, and leaned back in the seat and stared out at the traffic. We rode in silence for a while and when I turned I saw that Mr. Ulado was

90

gazing straight ahead while Mbwato was staring out of his window at whatever there was to see at 38th Street and Third Avenue. "The persons who have the shield have been in touch with you by now, I presume," he said, still looking out the window.

"Yes."

"I scarcely think that you would care to tell me what they have proposed?"

"No," I said. "I can't tell you that."

He turned from the window. "I didn't think that you would—or could, I suppose I should say. Nevertheless, I'm sure that you understand that I have to ask."

"I can understand that."

"I have exhausted all possibilities in Washington," he said.

"Possibilities for what?"

"For recognition of Komporeen by your country. You've probably noticed the rather bizarre clothing that Mr. Ulado and I are wearing. It would be most difficult not to notice."

"I've noticed," I said.

"Yes. Well, we grew weary of waiting in the outer offices of your State Department in our conservative lounge suits, virtually ignored not only by your officials with whom we had appointments, but also by their clerks. Native dress would have been far more appropriate (especially in that ghastly Washington weather), but it was unobtainable so we purchased these rather garish garments off the peg."

"It's a nice fit," I said.

Mbwato smiled. "They served their purpose. Rather than have us clutter up their reception rooms, your State Department officials no longer kept us waiting. Some of them were quite decent chaps, in fact. But it really made no difference. Their policy is set, their minds are closed, or at least made up. We even showed a motion-picture film to one of them, an assistant under-secretary of State for African Affairs."

"Littman Cox?" I said.

"Yes. Littman Cox. Do you know him?"

"No. I've just heard of him."

"I see. We had films flown in from Komporeen and in truth, Mr. St. Ives, they almost made me physically ill. They were films of our children as they literally starved to death before one's eyes. One child, a seven-year-old boy, died while the camera recorded it. He died of starvation while we watched. He starved because of the Jandolaean blockade. I thought that surely this would have some impact."

"Did it?"

Mbwato shook his head slowly from side to side and his eyes seemed to grow infinitely sad. "Your Mr. Cox said that it was terrible, but that there was nothing he could do. Then he thanked us for what he described as a 'most instructive morning' and excused himself to keep an important luncheon date. I must say that I found him rather ineffectual."

"I've heard him called worse," I said, remembering Myron Greene's comment. "But you didn't stop with an assistant under-secretary of State, did you? He has about as much influence as I do."

"No," Mbwato said. "We didn't stop with Mr. Cox. We ended with him. He was at the tail of what has proved to be a rather long line. In the two months that Mr. Ulado and I have been in the States—planning the theft of the shield, if all else failed—we have seen scores of your senators and congressmen, the secretaries of your Departments of State and Agriculture and Defense. We have even spent an hour with your Vice-President, and all have been personally sympathetic, but none has been encouraging. Our one port remains blockaded. The British have provided the Jandolaeans with radar-guided antiaircraft weaponry so that it is impossible to fly in supplies except at great risk, which only a few pilots are willing to take."

Ulado had turned in the front seat and was following the conversation closely, nodding his head in sharp little jerks when he felt that Mbwato had made a telling point. "I'm sorry," I said. "I wish there was something I could do. But there isn't."

Mbwato took a deep breath and let it out slowly. It was more than a sigh: it seemed to be the cautious physical response of a man who has something important to say, but who also knows that his anger and rage might make it come out all wrong. "There is something you can do, Mr. St. Ives. There is indeed. You can return the shield of Komporeen to us once it is in your possession. I have been authorized to raise your fee to seventy-five thousand dollars." There was no smile this time.

I shook my head. "I can't do that; you know I can't."

The four weeks of the Washington run-around seemed to bubble and then boil over. Mbwato fought it. I could see the muscles in his large face working as he tried to recover his poise, but it was no use. When he spoke it came out as a deep roar. I thought it was the pained outcry of a man to whose desperate need too many persons had already said no.

"Can't! Can't, you say. Goddamn it, man, that shield can save a country, a nation, a people, and you sit there and say 'I can't do that.' Let me tell you about starvation, St. Ives. Let me tell you what it's already done to more than 800,000 children in my country. During the first few days they have stomach cramps, horrible, intense pain. Then the stomach bloats while it shrinks in size. They cry for the first few days. They cry and they eat anything that will stop the horrible pain. They eat mud and grass and straw and chalk. Anything. And then they grow weaker, so weak that they can no longer cry, only whimper, and their breath begins to stink and smell like acetone because they're burning up their fat and they have no carbohydrates to replace it. Then, after this, they sink into lethargy and at least they can sleep. That's all they have left. Sleep and death. The proteins are gone now and their stomachs are distended and the degeneration of the kidneys and the liver sets in. If they're lucky, they'll

93

catch a disease which they can't fight and which will finish them off quickly. Even a slight infection from a cut or a scratch will do it. If they don't contract a disease or develop an infection, they just die—slowly and painfully. How much—how much do you want, St. Ives, to keep my nation's children alive? A hundred thousand? Is that your price? All right. I'll increase it to one hundred thousand. It's cheap really. With the shield we can hold out until recognition comes from France and Germany, and with the recognition will come food, and perhaps only another hundred thousand or so children will starve instead of another five hundred or seven hundred thousand. It's only a piece of brass to you, St. Ives. To my country, it's life itself."

Mbwato slumped back against the seat. He looked spent and utterly weary. I turned my head and stared out the window of the car at the well-fed pedestrians. Somehow they all seemed fat, almost blubbery. I didn't look at Mbwato when I spoke and I could feel the flush rising in my face.

"What you ask is impossible," I said, but it didn't seem to be me who was talking. It was some totally rational stranger. I didn't much care for him. "You're asking me to take a quarter of a million dollars of other people's money," the Rational Stranger said, "and turn it over to a gang of thieves. Then I'm to hand the shield over to you while you slip me a hundred thousand or seventy-five thousand under the table. That turns me into a thief, of course, and that's why I'm not going to do it. Because I'd get caught and go to jail and I don't want to go to jail. Not for you. Not for Komporeen. Not even for the kids that are starving to death. It's just not in me—do you understand? I just can't do it." The Rational Stranger hurried on. "All I can suggest is that you get the shield back from whoever stole it. Get it back anyway you can. Buy it back or steal it back. I don't care which. But I won't help you do that either."

I looked at Mbwato then and found that he was staring at me. There was dislike in his gaze; not hatred, just dislike. And there was also bitter contempt, enough to make the flush in my face start up again. But he was calm now and when he spoke his voice was as cold and as hard as frosted chrome. "Is it that you fear your reputation as a go-between will suffer, Mr. St. Ives? Let me assure you that you won't suffer nearly the agony that one child in Komporeen suffers as he starves to death."

The Cadillac had drawn up in front of my hotel, but I made no move to get out. Ulado was still turned in the front seat and his head jerked in agreement with Mbwato's last statement.

"I'm sorry," I said. "I just can't do it. I told you why and you'll simply have to accept it. I'm sorry." I reached for the handle of the door, but turned and looked at Mbwato again. He was staring at me and there was a half-smile on his face. Suddenly it became a full smile, that dazzling white-on-black smile that threatened to light up the world. He reached over and slapped me on the knee. "Don't be sorry, Mr. St. Ives. Don't ever be sorry about anything that you lack the courage to attempt, otherwise you will go through life with a burden of guilt that eventually will crush you."

"All right," I said, and again reached for the handle of the door.

"We'll be seeing more of each other," Mbwato said.

"I don't think so."

"Then you are mistaken."

"All right," I said again.

"Just one thing that struck me," he said.

"What?"

"When you were describing why you could not return the shield to us. It sounded as though your excuses were coming from the lips of one of your minor State Department officials." He smiled broadly as I opened the door and got out. "Good-by," he said. I merely nodded and watched the car as it drew away from the curb. Considering what Mbwato said he had just been through in Washington, he could probably think of no more cutting remark for a parting insult. And it may have been that there wasn't one.

9

The Rational Stranger took the elevator up to his ninth-floor de luxe efficiency, fetched a bottle of Scotch down from the cabinet above the Pullman sink, and poured himself a jumbo drink in the vain hope that it would help to erase the memory of the hopelessness and pain that seemed to have flickered in the eyes of Conception Mbwato.

It didn't, of course. It merely transformed the Rational Stranger into the Sententious Slob who stood by the window and looked down at the street while mouthing to himself such pithy aphorisms as "the master of action oft becomes the servant of regret" and "the fool thinks with his heart; the wise man with his mind." They weren't very good aphorisms, and the Scotch didn't help any, so I picked up the Manhattan directory and looked up the number and address of Frank Spellacy. There was only one Spellacy in the book and he had a Park Avenue address, which could mean something or nothing at all. I dialed the number and a man's voice answered on the second ring with "Mesa Verde Estates."

"Mr. Spellacy, please."

"This is Mr. Spellacy," the voice said, a pleasant, cheerful voice that seemed to be larded with great, fat streaks of sincerity. "My secretary's just stepped out for the institutional coffee break." He chuckled about that, as if he were gently tolerant of most of the world's foibles. "Now how can I help you?"

"I'd like to talk to you," I said. "This afternoon. My name's St. Ives. Philip St. Ives."

There was a moment's silence; perhaps half a moment, only a beat really, and then Spellacy's voice came over the phone again, still exuding its confidence, but tinged with a touch of regret. "I was just glancing at my appointment book, Mr. St. Ives, and it seems that I'm rather tied up this afternoon with a couple of important conferences. Perhaps we could make it later in the week—Friday would be good. Yes. Say Friday afternoon at three?"

"No. Friday at three's no good. This afternoon at four is fine."

"I just told you—"

"I know what you told me. A couple of important conferences. Postpone them."

"Look, Mr. St. John—"

"Ives," I said. "St. Ives."

"Ives then. I'm not in the habit of having strangers call me up and tell me how to run my business." He managed to get some real indignation into that.

"But I'm not exactly a stranger, am I? I believe we have some mutual friends. We have the art dealer, Mr. Albert Shippo, and that man about town, the noted sportsman, Mr. Johnny Parisi. In fact, I had dinner with Johnny just last night."

"You mention my name?" Spellacy said, and all the cheerfulness and goodwill were gone.

"That's something I thought we might talk about. This afternoon."

There was another pause, this time a long one, and then Spellacy said, "All right. Four o'clock. Here."

"At four," I said, and hung up.

I was boiling some water for a cup of tea and slicing up some cucumbers for a sandwich when I heard the knock at the door. The tomato soup and crackers hadn't been enough and I was hungry again. I had been half watching some English film on TV where the principals sat around drinking tea and eating cucumber sandwiches, which I happen to like, and it had provoked my appetite, but then I'm highly susceptible to fictional portrayals of food, whether written or filmed. In my youth the passages that Thomas Wolfe wrote about food had made me ravenous. And once, while reading Tom Lea's *The Brave Bulls*, I had put the book down, left my apartment, and walked four miles to find a Spanish-American store that sold canned tortillas and frijoles. Now I found myself craving a cucumber sandwich. I laid the knife on the minuscule drainboard, went to the door, and opened it. Lieutenant Kenneth Ogden of vice stood there, wearing one of his three-hundred-dollar suits and a smile that only made him look a little less angry than usual.

"Would you like a cucumber sandwich?" I said.

"A what?"

"A cucumber sandwich. Come on in."

He came in. "The trouble with you, St. Ives, is that you live alone. It's not natural. It's against nature and God."

"If you don't want a cucumber sandwich, would you like a drink? I've got Scotch, vodka, and bourbon."

"Bourbon," Ogden said. "And water."

I mixed him a bourbon and water and then went back to my sandwich. I cut the crusts off the bread, spread butter on both pieces, placed the cucumbers carefully on one slice, covered it with the other, and then cut it diagonally both ways into four parts—just like an old maid expecting an afternoon call from the vicar.

Ogden stood to one side and watched me work. I glanced at him once and there didn't seem to be any admiration in his gaze. I found the tea bags and placed one in a cup and poured it full of boiling water. When it had steeped enough I carried it and the cucumber sandwich over to my favorite chair and lowered myself into it carefully, holding the cup of tea in one hand, the cucumber sandwich in the other.

"You oughta get married again," he said. "Or get a job. Cucumber sandwiches at half-past two in the afternoon and the goddamned TV set on along with it. Christ." He moved over to the set and switched it off. "You're coming apart, Ives. Your seams are splitting."

"I like cucumbers," I said. "I also like tea and cucumber sandwiches." I took a bite and chewed it slowly. It didn't taste as good as I'd thought it would. If I could have eaten it alone while watching the actors in the English film eat their sandwiches, it probably would have tasted all right.

"What's on your mind?" I said.

Ogden took a small swallow of his drink. "That's good bourbon," he said.

"I wouldn't know," I said. "I don't drink bourbon. It's another one of my idiosyncrasies probably brought about by a monklike existence."

Ogden quit wandering around the room and sat in a chair opposite me. Although pushing fifty or five years past it, he wore his clothes well, but they did nothing to disguise the gray in his short-cropped hair or the lines in his face, all of which seemed to turn down, as if in constant disapproval. It was an oblong face, almost as wide at the chin as it was at the forehead. It was also a tough face, a hard one, which had heard all the lies and witnessed all the depravity that New York had to offer. His Captain Easy nose, a little red at the tip, snuffled every few minutes as if he had just smelled something rotten but couldn't quite tell what it was. The eyes that looked at me over the rim of his glass were blue with all the color and warmth of a dreary day in February.

"How's your daughter?" I said, and took a sip of my tea.

"Next month. She starts next month."

"Where?"

"Ohio State. I'm going to drive her out."

"It's a good school."

"Yeah. That's what I hear. God knows, it costs enough."

"Why didn't she go closer to home?"

Ogden waved his left hand. "Ah, Christ, you know kids. They don't wanta stay home and go to college. They wanta get away, out of the state somewhere, at least out of town. That's half of it, I guess."

"I suppose," I said, and took another bite of my sandwich. "So what brings you around here at two-thirty of an afternoon when you're supposed to be out rousting vice lords, if that's what they still call them?"

"I been hearing some things," he said.

"From where, Washington? From Demeter?"

"He called Monday. He wanted to know about you. I said you were okay, just a little careful."

"I thought you told him cautious."

"Maybe I did. I don't remember. Careful, cautious, it doesn't matter."

"Did he tell you what I was on?"

"Yeah. Some kind of shield. African. You're trying to buy it back for two hundred and fifty thousand. Some shield."

"It has quite a history."

"Demeter seemed to think you could use a little help."

"Are you offering?"

Ogden drained his drink and placed it on the carpet beside his chair because there wasn't any table handy. "Not officially."

"Unofficially?"

"If you think you need it."

"I don't."

He shrugged. "I just thought I might do a little moonlighting. I got a day off tomorrow."

"What makes tomorrow so special?"

"I hear that's when you buy it back."

"You hear from whom?"

He smiled for the first time. His teeth were white and regular and even. Too white and regular and even. They were false. I felt better, somehow glad that Ogden wore false teeth, or dentures, as the television ads insisted on calling them. It made him more vulnerable. Ogden closed his lips quickly, turning off the smile as if he were concerned that I might notice the teeth.

"When you're a cop for twenty-three years you hear things," he said. "Now when you used to be on the paper, you used to hear things, didn't you? You know, some jerk would call up with an anonymous tip and then you, knowing he was a jerk, would still go ahead and check it out and find that he was telling the truth after all. Well, let's say it was something like that. Accidental like."

"Why did Demeter call you?"

"We're old pals. We went to the FBI academy together. In 'fifty-four."

"I don't buy that anonymous-tip business," I said.

Ogden cocked one eyebrow at me; his left one. It was a polite enough expression and its tone carried over into his voice. "Don't you now?"

"No, I don't. I think that after Demeter called and told you how high the payoff was you started to check with every pigeon in town. Maybe you found one that knew something, not much, but something, enough for you to figure that you could cut yourself a slice of the pie. Not a big slice probably, but something that would make sacrificing a day off worthwhile. How much did you have in mind?"

Ogden smiled again, but this time he kept his lips

together. "Let's say that what you say is true. Now I'm not saying it is, but if it was, then I'd say that five thousand would be just about right."

"And just what would you do to earn it?"

"I'd help keep you alive, St. Ives. Now that oughta be worth five grand to you, if not to anybody else."

"Do you know who the thieves are?"

Ogden shook his head. "No, I don't and that's the truth. I just hear that the switch will take place tomorrow and that they play a little rough sometimes— whoever they are."

This time I smiled at him. I tried to make it friendly; I'm not sure that I succeeded. "Or it could have been another way, couldn't it? It could have been that you called Demeter down in Washington about an hour or two ago and Demeter had just talked to Frances Wingo of the museum who'd told him that the switch will take place tomorrow. That's all you really needed to know, wasn't it? Then your mind starts working and you figure a way to cut yourself in. For five thousand—on your day off. So you drop by here with a story about how rough the thieves play, which is supposed to turn me into a lump of Jell-o, and I agree to pay you five thousand dollars for whatever protection you can give me tomorrow. Now, it could have been like that, couldn't it, Ken?"

Ogden shook his head sadly. "I feel sorry for you, St. Ives."

"Why? Because of my suspicious nature?"

He rose from his chair. "One of these days you're going to play it too safe, too careful, too cautious. One of these days you're not going to trust somebody when you should, then pffft! No more St. Ives."

I put the empty teacup and sandwich plate on the floor and rose. "But that's not today, is it?"

Ogden picked up his Borsalino hat from the hexagonal table and brushed it against the sleeve covering his left arm. "Not today, maybe. Maybe not even tomorrow. But sometime soon." He put his hat on his head, tilted it slightly to the left, gave me the opportunity to examine his false teeth again, said "Thanks for the drink" and left. I went over and picked up his glass and my dirty dishes and put them in the sink where I began to wash them slowly, as neat and as tidy as the old maid after the vicar has left.

It was a respectable enough building twenty-nine stories high that had been designed by some long-forgotten architect who apparently had never heard of the Bauhaus. It looked like what it was, an office building on Park Avenue where people went to work in the morning at nine and left at five after having sold or bought or traded or even created something, perhaps an advertisement for a new cemetery. The directory in the marble lobby said that Mesa Verde Estates was on the eleventh floor. I looked at my watch and it was three minutes before four so I got in one of the automatic elevators along with a stenographer who was carrying a white paper bag that was brown around the bottom where the coffee had slopped out of the paper cups. She got off at six; I got off at eleven.

Mesa Verde Estates was in 1106, which turned out to be four doors to my left from the elevator. A sign on the door of 1106 read MESA VERDE ESTATES, FRANK SPELLACY, PRESIDENT. I knocked, and when no one said "come in" or "who's there" or even "go away" I tried the doorknob. It turned easily so I pushed the door open and walked in. It was a medium-sized office, big enough for two persons perhaps, a man and his secretary, if he wasn't worried about privacy. Green steel shelves lined one side of the office, the left side, and they were choked with what seemed to be four-color brochures advertising Mesa Verde Estates. There were three windows at the rear of the office and their venetian blinds were half up, so that the light from the afternoon sun spilled onto the large executive desk that was placed in front of the windows. Three leather arm chairs were arranged in front of the desk. The floor was carpeted with some speck-led brown and black synthetic fiber. On the right wall were some handsome color photos of desert scenes, four of them. Below them was a couch and a glass-topped coffee table. There was no secretarial desk or typewriter, only the executive walnut desk that had a high-backed judge's chair behind it. A man sat in the chair, but the upper part of his body was bent over the desk, his bald head resting on a green blotter, his left arm extended toward a beige telephone, his left hand clutching a yellow pencil. I walked over to the desk and looked at him. The blotter was trying to soak up all of the blood, but it wasn't doing too well. I reached over and felt for a pulse in the wrist of the hand that clutched the pencil; there was none. The phone rang and I jumped. It rang seven times before it quit. Frank Spellacy was too dead to hear it.

He had been a plumpish man, dressed in a gray pin-striped suit. Gold-rimmed glasses still rested on a thick nose. His eyes were closed and his mouth was slightly open and I almost expected to hear him snore. He was around fifty and the sun, beating in from the windows, made his bald head seem pinker than it really was. Underneath the hand that held the pencil was a small white pad. He had written something on the pad, one word. From the way the letters straggled and ran together, he may have written it as he sat there, half sprawled over his desk, dying. There was only the one word and I read it upside down. The one word was "Wingo."

105

10

There seemed to be no reason for what I did next, no reason other than that I felt that the one word, the name, scrawled on the white pad by a dying man, was meant for me. It was mine, so I took it. I pulled the pad from underneath the lifeless hand that still clutched the Eberhard Faber yellow pencil and slipped it into my jacket pocket. And then, remembering lessons learned from five thousand hours before the tube and perhaps from another three thousand or so in darkened buildings that sold sustenance (popcorn) along with escape, I took out my handkerchief and used it to shield my palm and fingers from the doorknob. In the hall I looked around and then hastily wiped the outside doorknob, found the stairs, scurried down two flights, rang for the elevator, waited and fretted, and then tried to look nondescript to the three passengers who were already aboard when it finally came and also to the three others who got on at the seventh, fourth, and third floors.

Outside, the Nickerson Building looked just like

what it was, an ordinary office building, perhaps 43 years old or older, built in the late 1920's on Park Avenue by a contractor who was doubtless dead by now, as dead as Frank Spellacy, and designed by an architect who didn't give a damn about Mies van der Rohe or Walter Gropius or even the infamous Marcel Breuer, who had threatened to saddle Grand Central Terminal with a 55-story mega-structure, which I could have inspected if I cared to look over my shoulder, which I didn't. Instead I walked quickly down Park Avenue for two blocks and then turned right, looking for a bar, any bar.

It was an ordinary place called The Cold Duck or The Green Rooster or something like that. The bar itself ran along the right-hand side and there were some tables and booths and checkered tablecloths and Chianti bottles that held half-burned candles. It was ten minutes after four and only a couple of dedicated topers were in attendance. I sat at the bar's far end, near the door, away from the drinkers, and when the bartender waddled down my way I ordered a double Scotch.

"What kind?" he said.

"Bar Scotch."

"On the rocks?"

"Just a straight shot with a glass of water."

I should have told him to serve it in a large glass because when I picked it up my hand shook so that it sloshed a little of the whisky over the rim, which chattered against my teeth. But I got it down, all of it down in two gulps, and then I signaled the bartender. He was in a deep conversation with the two tipplers, talking learnedly, no doubt, of sports or cars or politics, or whatever drunks and bartenders talk about at four in the afternoon, and he seemed reluctant to come all the way down to where I sat, or it may have been that his feet hurt.

"Another double?" he said.

"Make it a single. Where's your phone?"

107

He jerked a thumb over his shoulder. "In the back, near the men's john."

I didn't even have to search for a dime on the way to the phone. I just picked it up, dialed 911, and when the voice answered—a policeman's voice—I said, "I'm only going to say this once. There's a dead man in room 1106 in the Nickerson Building on Park Avenue. His name's Frank Spellacy. S-p-e-l-l-a-c-y. Spellacy." Then I hung up.

The drink was waiting for me when I went back to my end of the bar. I didn't really want it but it was there so I drank it, put three one-dollar bills and some change next to the empty glass, and left. I caught a cab back to the Adelphi and once there, up in my de luxe efficiency on the ninth floor with its Pullman kitchen and its yellow-tiled bathroom, I took the pad from my pocket, the pad with the one-word, one-name message on it, and read it for the first time right side up. It still said Wingo. I tore the page off the pad, ripped it into small pieces, and flushed it down the toilet. Still remembering lessons well learned from screens both large and small, I tore the rest of the pad up and spent five minutes in the bathroom flushing the toilet six times. There was a cardboard backing for the pad, but it seemed too much trouble to tear up, so I tossed it into the wastebasket.

I slumped into my favorite chair, the one where scarcely two hours before I had been eating a cucumber sandwich, drinking a cup of tea, and demonstrating to a New York cop on the make just how smart I really was. I wondered about that for a while. When I discovered a dead man, a small-time grifter, in his office, killed by either a knife or a gun, I stole the one-word message that he used up his life writing because with magnificent egoism, I assumed that it was meant for me. Not for his wife or children or even the cops, but for me, someone he didn't know, someone he had spoken to once, over the telephone, for forty-five seconds, perhaps a minute. That proved how smart I was. And instead of calling the police and reporting the murder, if that's what it was, and waiting for them to get there and giving them all the information that I could, which might possibly have helped them find whoever killed the man, the small-time grifter who sold desert lots for ten dollars down and ten dollars a month, and then probably discounted the paper to some finance company, I instead acted like a fool who ran when he should stay and stayed when he should run. I was smart all right. Even brilliant. No wonder the country was going to hell.

I sat there in my favorite chair, smoking a cigarette and brooding and thinking about the one-word message that Spellacy had left for someone, possibly me, but probably not. I spent fifteen minutes thinking about it and then I picked up the phone and dialed O for long distance.

When she came on I told her that I would like to call the Coroner's Office in Washington, D.C. There was some more palaver while she asked whom I wished to speak to and finally I told her that I would like to speak to the coroner himself, but would settle for whoever answered the phone. A man's voice answered with "Coroner's Office."

I told him my name and then asked, "If a man were killed in an automobile accident, would he immediately come under your jurisdiction?"

"Yes, he would," the good solid civil-service voice said.

"Would you perform an autopsy?"

"Yes, that's automatically done in accidents, homicides, suicides, and what-have-you."

I didn't ask him what a what-have-you was, although it seemed to take in a lot of territory. But he wasn't through yet; he warmed to his subject. "Now in the case of illness, if the deceased hasn't seen a doctor or been attended by one within the last ten days, an autopsy is automatically performed. That also holds true if the deceased has not been seen by anyone— you know, vanished—for a period of twenty-four hours or more prior to his death."

"I'd like to get some information on a man who was killed in a car wreck about four weeks ago."

"Are you the next of kin?" the civil-service voice said.

"No. I'm a reporter. With *The New York Times*." There was no use in going second class.

The voice relented a little. "What was the deceased's name?"

"Wingo," I said.

"His first name?"

That wrecked it. "Well, we haven't been able to find out his first name. He died under rather mysterious circumstances."

There was a pause at the Washington end, at the District of Columbia's Coroner's Office at 19th and E Streets, Southeast. It was a long, chilly pause. "I'm sorry, but in such cases the next of kin must grant permission for the release of such information."

"Well, thanks anyway."

He said that I was welcome, but I don't think he really meant it.

I sat there in the chair with my hand on the phone thinking about all the influential persons that I knew in Washington who could pry the information out of the Coroner's Office without going to the next of kin. For some reason I didn't think that Frances Wingo would appreciate my attempt to find out why she had become a widow. But the influential persons whom I knew were probably too busy or too inept to get the information today and I was too impatient to wait for tomorrow so I called Myron Greene, the lawyer.

"I need a favor," I told him after we said hello and he informed me that Spivack had deposited the check from the Coulter Museum.

"What kind of a favor?" Myron Greene said, and there seemed to be suspicion and distrust in his voice, but that was really how he always talked.

"I need to get a coroner's report in Washington so I can find out how somebody died."

"That takes the permission of the next of kin," Myron Greene said.

"I know. I've already tried. That's why I'm calling you. I need the information this afternoon."

"That's impossible."

"No it isn't, Myron, not for you, it isn't. You have the influence down there and I don't. That's why I called."

"I'm sorry, but I'm just too busy. Maybe I can do something tomorrow."

"If I don't get the information this afternoon, or this evening at the latest, then I'm walking off this thing."

"What's that—what's that?" Myron Greene said, and began to wheeze at me over the phone.

"I'm through. Finished. Somebody else can get the shield back."

"Something's happened," he said. "What's happened? I have a right to know. I have every right—"

"Somebody else has been killed."

"Who?"

"The name would mean nothing to you."

"Was he connected with the . . . the thieves?"

"I don't know. But he probably knew who they were."

"God damn it, St. Ives, can't you ever tell anything straight?"

"Get me the information I want and I'll tell you the entire story. You may get to be a criminal lawyer after all. If I don't get the information, it's as I said. I quit. Now. This afternoon."

Myron Greene gave me a long wheezy sigh. "Well, there's one possibility. A good friend of mine is now an assistant U.S. attorney down there. He could probably get it."

"This afternoon?"

"If *I* asked him. He was a year behind me at school."

"Ask him."

"What do you want exactly?"

"I want to know the cause of death of a man named Wingo. He supposedly was killed in a car accident about four weeks ago."

"Wingo? Isn't that the name of the woman who—"

"The same."

"Her husband?"

"Yes."

"Do you think that she—"

I interrupted him. "I don't think anything, Myron. I'm just trying to find out what to think."

"All right, all right. What's his first name?"

"I don't know."

"Christ."

"There shouldn't be too many Wingos who died in a car wreck four weeks ago. Just have your friend find out what the autopsy says."

Myron Greene was silent for a moment, except for a couple of wheezes. "Is this just a hunch on your part or do you think you really have something?"

"I don't have a thing," I said. "It's just a hunch."

"I'll be back to you," Myron Greene said, and hung up.

Myron Greene called back at six thirty-five that evening.

"I've missed my train," he said. "Margaret will be furious." Margaret was his wife.

"Want me to call her?"

"No, I don't want you to call her. She thinks you're a—a bad influence."

"She's probably right."

"That hunch you had."

"What about it?"

"It seems to have paid off."

"How?"

Myron Greene was excited. I could tell from the way that his wheezes rasped over the phone in short, quick bursts as he fought for breath. "Just take it easy, Myron," I said. "Try for a deep breath."

He was silent for a moment, as if holding his breath, and then there was a long, shuddering wheeze. "I talked to my friend," he said in between the next gasp. "He called the Coroner's Office. They didn't like the idea of giving out the information, but he was persuasive."

"What did he get?"

"On July 26th, George Compton Wingo, 44, was found dead in a one-car automobile accident on Circumferential Highway 495 near exit 13. That's in Virginia. The automobile, a new Chevrolet Impala, was a total loss." Myron Greene sounded as if he were reading from notes and he paused to wheeze a couple of times.

"An autopsy," he went on, "was performed on July 27th and it was determined that Wingo was already dead when his car turned over three times as it rolled down an embankment. He had died several hours earlier from a massive overdose of heroin."

"Was he hooked?" I said.

"I beg your pardon."

"Was he a habitual user?"

"Oh. Multiple punctures in both his left and right arms indicated that he was a habitual user of narcotics, probably heroin."

"Is that all?"

"Isn't that enough?"

"Almost," I said. "Almost. Myron, do me another favor, will you?"

"What now?"

"Take a cab home to Darien and put it on my bill."

11

Frances Wingo was prompt. She knocked on my door at two thirty-five the following day, Thursday, which meant that she had flown by private plane or had caught the one o'clock shuttle from Washington and that it had had no trouble landing and that taxis had been plentiful at LaGuardia.

"Come in," I said.

"Thank you." She came in, carrying with some difficulty an inexpensive man's two-suiter in her left hand. A striped blue and white raincoat was draped over her right arm.

"Heavy?" I said, reaching for the suitcase.

She let me have it, a little reluctantly, I thought. "Heavy," she said. I turned in the room, wondering where to put the suitcase, which seemed to weigh between 55 and 60 pounds. I finally decided to put it in the tub in the bathroom. Before I put it there, I weighed it on the scale. Fifty-eight pounds.

When I came back out she said, "Why there?"

"I don't know," I said. "Maybe it's because it would be the last place I would look if I were looking for it."

"Aren't you going to count it?"

"Did you?"

"No."

"Did you look at it?"

"Yes."

"Pretty?"

"Not particularly."

"Since you don't care much for money, maybe you'd care for a drink."

"I think I would."

"Bourbon or Scotch?"

"Bourbon."

"Pick out a chair," I said. "Or the couch. They're all about the same."

"Thank you." She draped her raincoat over a wing-backed chair and sank into it. She wore a blue dress that was neither too complicated nor too simple, blue shoes that seemed to both match and complement the dress, and in her lap she held a blue purse that seemed to be made of the same leather as the shoes. When I turned from mixing the drinks she was slowly surveying the room and she managed not to grimace at the prints on the wall, which had been supplied by the color-blind management of the Adelphi.

"Horrible, aren't they?" I said as I handed her a drink.

"A bit."

"The management's choice."

"Not yours?"

"No. I'm still hung up on Maxfield Parrish."

"He was 96 when he died. In 1966."

"Do you like Parrish?" I said.

"No. Do you?"

"Probably because I know I shouldn't."

"Double reverse snobbism."

"Really? I never thought of it like that." I was seated on the couch opposite her. I put my drink on

115

the glass-topped coffee table and lit a cigarette. "I'm sorry you couldn't make it for lunch."

She didn't bother to make an excuse. "Will you get it back today?"

"I don't know."

"Haven't they been in touch with you again?"

"No."

"Will they?"

"I don't know."

"What do you plan to do, or do you believe in plans?"

I took a swallow of my drink. "I'm going to rent a car. I don't own a car, you know. I'm going to rent a car and drive to the third Howard Johnson on the Jersey Turnpike. I'm going to check in by six o'clock this evening accompanied by fifty-eight pounds of used tens and twenties. I will sit by the phone until they tell me what they want me to do. Then I will do precisely that because if I don't, I could wind up just like your husband. Dead."

She was either a very good actress or she didn't know what I was talking about. "I'm afraid you've lost me, Mr. St. Ives. What does my husband have to do—or what connection is there between his death and the shield?" There wasn't a blink, or a tremor, or even that oversupply of calmness which most good liars have. She merely sat there, a politely interested look on her face, as if she had just asked whether I thought she should take the four or the five o'clock shuttle back to Washington.

"Your husband was an addict. A junkie. He didn't die from the wreck he was in. He died from a massive overdose of heroin."

That didn't bother her either. She smiled slightly; it was a cool, almost pitying smile. "You seem inordinately interested in my husband, Mr. St. Ives. Why?"

"Maybe I'm interested in knowing what kind of man would marry someone like you. Or rather, what kind of man would you consent to marry. Somehow a junkie doesn't fit."

"Is it really any of your business?"

I put my drink down on the glass-topped table with a clatter. "You're damned right it's my business. One person has already died because of this shield, two if you count his wife who hanged herself. Now with your husband dead from an overdose of heroin, I think the score is now three dead and I don't want me to make it four." I purposely left out Spellacy, although his death would have helped to run up the total.

"You do become belligerent, don't you?"

"It's only one of many failings."

"You should try to correct it."

"I'll work on it this fall. You think group therapy might help?"

"I'm sure it would do you a world of good."

"You knew he was an addict?"

"Yes," she said. "I knew. It would be most difficult not to know."

"Where'd he get it?"

"I never inquired."

"How'd he pay for it?"

"May I have one of your cigarettes? I quit smoking three years ago, but—" If this was a crack in her composure, it was a small one. She sat in the wingbacked chair, the barely tasted drink on a table, her hands folded over the blue purse in her lap. I rose and offered her a cigarette and lit it for her. She inhaled deeply and then blew the smoke out in a thin stream.

"Silly, isn't it?"

"What?"

"Wanting something like that suddenly, wanting it so bad that—well, never mind." She inhaled some more smoke and blew it out. "I'm going to tell you about my husband, Mr. St. Ives. I'm going to tell you about him because I don't want you poking around in

117

my life. There are too many snoops abroad in the land today who seem bent on destroying privacy. I resent it. I wholeheartedly subscribe to the right to be let alone, as someone phrased it several years ago. So after I tell you about my husband, I sincerely hope that you will do just that—let me alone."

She paused, as if expecting me to assure her that I would take the next plane to El Paso and never come back once she had told me about her husband. I only nodded.

"My husband, before he became addicted, was not only a brilliant artist, he was also—or could have been—one of the nation's leading museum directors or curators. He studied with Paul Sachs at the Fogg Art Museum at Harvard in the early 1940's. He was very young then, no more than a precocious sixteen or seventeen, and in 1943 he joined the Marines and saw action as a combat artist, I think they called them, at Iwo Jima, where he did an unusually good series of watercolors which were reproduced in *Life* and which brought him nationwide attention. After his discharge from the Marines he was offered a post as director of a small but good museum in the Midwest. From there he went to a better position in Chicago and then to New York as head of a private museum. It doesn't matter to you which one, does it?"

"No," I said. "It doesn't."

"We met here in New York at some party. I had wanted to paint, but I wasn't good enough to be good and I had enough sense to realize it. So I did the next best thing. I turned to museum work. George was extremely helpful. He was painting almost every spare moment that he could find and he was good. Terribly good. Some of his friends who had seen his work begged him to hold an exhibition, but he always refused, claiming that the time wasn't quite right. When I finished my studies we were married and I was appointed director of a small museum here in New York

—largely on George's recommendation. A few years later the offer came from the Coulter Museum. He turned it down."

"He?" I said.

"Yes. They wanted George. He recommended me. Strongly. And with a few misgivings on Mr. Spencer's part, I was hired."

"Why did he turn it down?"

She shrugged. "He'd decided that he no longer was interested in museum work. He wanted to paint full time. I agreed, of course, and we moved to Washington. The salary was more than adequate and for a while things worked out quite well."

"Then what?"

"George went into a deep depression. He stopped painting, drank too much, sometimes disappeared for days at a time. Finally, about a year and a half ago, he told me that he was addicted to heroin. I don't know when it really began; he would never tell me."

"How big was his habit?"

"I don't know."

"All right. How much did it cost him a day?"

"Toward the end it was around two hundred dollars."

"Where did he get it?"

"He sold his paintings. All of them, one by one. They brought very good prices. As I said, he was brilliant."

"But he finally ran out of paintings."

"Yes."

"Then what?"

"I gave him money."

"For how long?"

"Several months."

"Until it ran out?"

"Yes."

"Then?"

"Then one day he said that he didn't need any more

money. That he'd found a private supply of heroin."

"When was this?"

"Two months ago, perhaps two and a half months."

"How many people knew about it?"

"About what?"

"His addiction."

"Not many. His doctor. A few old friends who'd moved to Washington when Kennedy was elected. Mr. Spencer. I told him; I thought it only fair."

"What did Spencer say?"

"He was most understanding and sympathetic. He even offered to pay for George's treatment in a private sanitarium."

"What happened?"

"George refused."

"What did Spencer say then?"

"Nothing. He never mentioned it again."

"And that's all who knew—a few friends and Spencer?"

"Yes."

"There was somebody else," I said.

"Who?"

"The guy who furnished the private supply."

12

Frances Wingo left at three-fifteen to catch the four o'clock shuttle back to Washington. At the door, just before she left, she turned and said, "You really do think my husband was somehow connected with the theft of the shield, don't you?"

"Yes. I thought I'd made that plain."

"How?"

"How was he connected?"

"Yes."

"I don't know," I said. "I have an idea, but I'm not sure. I don't really know that I'll ever be sure."

"It has something to do with the guard, the one who was killed, hasn't it?"

"I think so."

"Will you tell me what your theory is?"

"No, because right now that's all it is, just a theory."

"And if it becomes more than a theory?"

"Then I'll tell you; if you still want to know."

She looked at me carefully for several seconds. "I

assure you, Mr. St. Ives, I will want to know. Very much."

"All right," I said.

"And you'll let me know what happens this evening?"

"Yes."

"Call me at home," she said. "I'll give you my number."

She gave me her number and I wrote it down. "I would walk you to the elevator," I said, "but I don't want to leave the suitcase by itself."

"That's quite all right. Good-by, Mr. St. Ives."

"Good-by."

I stood in the doorway and watched her walk down the hall, a tall, blond woman with short-cropped hair, a widow of four weeks who now could cry herself to sleep every night because her husband, brilliant but dead, had been not only a junkie, but probably the accomplice of thieves. There was, I decided, a lot of waste in the world.

I was not as blasé about the suitcase and its contents as I had pretended to be before Frances Wingo. Despite inflation, a quarter of a million dollars was still a fortune to me, an immense one, and I was always amazed that those who used my services could raise such staggering sums so easily. If someone were to kidnap my kindergarten-bound son, I could, thanks to the check from the Coulter Museum, scrape up fifteen thousand, but not a dime more. My son, it seemed, was safe unless his new stepfather turned out to be embarrassingly wealthy, which, knowing my ex-wife, was not at all unlikely.

I took the suitcase out of the tub and carried it to the bed. The case wasn't locked so I opened it and stood there for long moments staring at a quarter of a million dollars in used tens and twenties, all carefully wrapped in brown paper bands which said that each bundle contained five hundred dollars. I didn't count it. I didn't even touch it. Winfield Spencer's Washington bank had already counted it and when it comes to sums like that, banks make no mistakes.

At four o'clock I drove out of the Avis garage in a rented four-door Plymouth and fought my way to the New Jersey Turnpike, which is, in my opinion, the most unlovely strip of superhighway in the nation. It's also a road that demands grim defensive driving fulfilled by either members of the Teamsters Union who like to let their twenty tons of steel nibble at your rear bumper or by the lane jumpers who flit back and forth, oblivious of their rear-view mirrors, ignorant of their directional signals. Most of the vehicles, I noticed, wore New Jersey license plates.

At 5:15 I turned into the third Howard Johnson motel and restaurant, which, like the rest of its breed, was all orange and white and dyspeptic-looking. I was handed a key to room 143 in exchange for $16 plus tax, got back in the car, drove past 143, and parked in front of 135. I unlocked the trunk, took out the suitcase, and walked back to 143. There was nothing in the motel room that I hadn't expected. There was a bed and a dresser and some chairs and a 21-inch television set (black and white) and some lamps and a carpet. Everything was either nailed down or securely fastened so that it couldn't be carted off at three o'clock in the morning. I looked in the bathroom and saw that it contained the usual equipment fashioned out of bright blue tile. I came out of the bathroom and placed the suitcase in a closet. Then I stretched out on the bed and waited for the phone to ring so that I could give somebody a quarter of a million dollars in exchange for a 68-pound brass shield that was at least 1,000 years old or older, or about as old as I felt.

When the phone rang I looked at my watch. It was exactly six o'clock and the voice on the phone belonged to the woman who had called me what now seemed to be a long time ago, a couple of years back, at the Madison Hotel in Washington. She then had

123

sounded as if she were reading the words that she had to say to me, but now the conversation was informal, almost chatty.

"You follow instructions very well, don't you, Mr. St. Ives?"

"What about the shield?"

"Is that really money in the suitcase that you carried into your room?"

"It's money."

"It's such a lot of money, isn't it?"

"The shield," I said.

She giggled then. It was a high-pitched giggle that went on for a long time and made her sound like a preadolescent girl who has heard her first dirty joke and found it to be quite funny. "The shield of Kompo-reen." She had lowered her voice and tried to make it as dramatic as possible, but she wasn't a very good actress and the effect wasn't humorous, only embarrassing, which she seemed to realize because she giggled again.

"The shield," I said, as patiently as I could, as if talking to a drunken friend who thought it would be a splendid idea to seek out some after-hours joints now that it was four o'clock in the morning and the bars were closed.

She said something then, not to me, but to someone else who was there with her wherever she was, next door in room 141 for all I knew. I couldn't understand what she said, but when she came back on the phone, she sounded as if she were reading again, although her voice was a little more singsong than before, as though she was trying to burlesque the whole thing.

"The exchange will not be made tonight. You will go to Washington tomorrow and check into the Madison Hotel by noon. At twelve-thirty you will receive further instructions. Do you want this repeated?"

"No," I said. "I don't want it repeated; all I want is the shield."

"Tomorrow, Mr. St. Ives," she said, again bringing

124

her voice down into that pseudodramatic register. "Tomorrow you will have the shield of Komp-o-reen." Then she giggled again for what seemed to be a long time and hung up.

I sat there on the edge of Mr. Howard Johnson's overly soft bed and wondered if I was too old to enroll in an International Correspondence School course, one that would teach me to be a bookkeeper or a draftsman or a sheet-metal mechanic. Earn big pay. Learn in your spare time. That was something that I had a lot of. I had eighteen hours before I had to be in Washington, before I had to talk to Giggles again or to her friend with the cottony voice. I could probably get halfway through lesson one before then.

I tried to recall the woman's voice. It hadn't been Bryn Mawr nor had it been East Side New York nor magnolia southern. It was just the voice of some female who probably had made it through high school and who thought that $250,000 was a great deal of money and who was willing to be mixed up in two or three murders to make sure that she got her share.

The giggle bothered me. I had heard people giggle like that before when they were high on pot or heroin, although with heroin there usually were more beatific smiles than giggles. Or she could have been slightly drunk except that there had been no slur in her voice, that voice with the All-American California-Midwest accent which could have belonged to someone who was 20 or 30 or a what-the-hell 40.

I took some foresight out of my jacket pocket, a half pint of J&B, and went into the bathroom where I struggled with the sanitary wrapping on a water glass. I poured some of the whisky into the glass, added water, went back into the bedroom, checked the closet to make sure that the suitcase was still there, and sat back down on the edge of the bed to brood some more.

The thieves could have worked it a half-dozen ways, I decided. Both of them could have followed me from New York and called from a pay phone. Or they could have checked into the motel that morning and watched me arrive. Or one of them, the man with the voice that sounded as if he had a mouthful of Band-Aids, could have sat in a parked car, followed my movements through his sunglasses, called the woman, and had her telephone me from their twelve-room duplex on East 62nd Street where she lolled around on the chaise longue while eating hashish-flavored bonbons. Only that didn't wash because she, had talked to somebody when she called me, and it was probably the man with the cottony voice. Or the cat.

My theories had all the substance of a badly spun cobweb so I put down my drink, picked up the phone, and placed a long-distance call to Frances Wingo in Washington. When she came on I said, "This is Philip St. Ives. It was a dry run."

"You didn't get the shield?"

"No."

"But you still have the money?"

"Yes, I still have it."

"What happened?"

"They tested me to see how well I follow instructions. They're to get in touch by twelve-thirty tomorrow in Washington at the Madison Hotel. You can do me a favor and make me a reservation."

"Yes, I will," she said. "But what happened?"

"I drove to the motel and checked in just like they instructed. A woman called at six, giggled a little, and then told me to be at the Madison tomorrow."

"Giggled?"

"She seemed to think it was all very funny."

"I don't understand."

"Neither do I. But I have no choice except to do what they say."

"I'll call Mr. Spencer and tell him what's happened," she said.

"All right."

"He's growing quite concerned, you know."

"So am I. You can tell him that I'm just as concerned as he is."

"Yes," she said, "I can imagine that you are." For the first time the tone of her voice edged up above the freezing mark. Not warm yet, but at least some of the chill was gone. "Why do you think they want you back in Washington?"

"I assume that's where the shield is," I said. "I also assume that's where it's always been. I don't think it ever left Washington. It's not something that one would like to lug around part of Manhattan and half of New Jersey."

"What do you think the chances are for recovering the shield tomorrow? Mr. Spencer will ask."

"I don't know. They're being awfully cagey, but they're running out of time. I'd guess that there's a fifty-fifty chance. No better."

"When will you call tomorrow?"

"When I get the shield back. Or when I'm sure that I won't get it."

"Do you want me to call Lieutenant Demeter?"

I thought about that for a moment. "No, don't call him. I'll talk to him myself tomorrow."

We said good-by and I replaced the phone and looked at my watch. It was six-thirty and because I could see no future in fighting the rush-hour traffic, I decided not to leave until seven. I mixed another drink and turned on the television set to a news program which did nothing to cheer me up, but at least gave me the consolation, for whatever it was worth, that a very large number of persons all over the world also had problems, most of which were worse than mine.

At seven I turned the set off, put the key to the room on the dresser, got the suitcase out of the closet, and headed for the rented car. It was still light, daylight-saving-time light, but he materialized at my elbow as if by some kind of magic just as I slammed the lid on

127

the trunk where I'd stored the suitcase.

"Good evening, Mr. St. Ives."

I turned to look at him. He was wearing a severely cut dark blue suit, white shirt, and a tie that just missed being bashful.

"Ah, the ubiquitous Mr. Ulado. I almost didn't recognize you in your new suit."

He smiled and fingered the knot in his tie. "We decided that our other garments had served their purpose."

"By we, I suppose you mean you and Mr. Mbwato, who must be lurking nearby."

"Surely not lurking, Mr. St. Ives."

"It's a good word and I haven't had the chance to use it in a long time. Or 'stealthily.' Another good word that I seldom have the chance to use. It describes the way you move, Mr. Ulado. Where were you hiding, up on the roof?"

"I was waiting behind the next car for you to come out or for the shield to go in."

"You must be disappointed."

Ulado smiled politely at that. "If you have a few moments, Mr. Mbwato would like to visit you."

"No gun this time?"

"No gun, Mr. St. Ives. Not even a fountain pen."

"And where is Mr. Mbwato?"

"Just around the corner."

"I suggest that if Mr. Mbwato wants to talk to me, he can come here. I don't like to leave my car unattended."

"Or the $250,000 in its trunk," Ulado said, smiling again.

"There's that, too."

Ulado nodded and disappeared around the corner of the motel. In a few moments the black rented seven-passenger Cadillac drew up alongside my car and the rear door opened. I climbed in and once again Mbwato's huge presence seemed to transform the Cadillac into an overcrowded Volkswagen.

128

"Good evening to you, Mr. St. Ives," he said. He was wearing a medium gray mohair suit, white shirt, and dark blue tie, and the complete outfit had cost him no more than five hundred dollars. They might be starving in Komporeen, I thought, but they still managed to send their emissaries out into the world well draped and well shod.

"I haven't got the shield," I said.

"So Mr. Ulado informs me. Pity, isn't it?"

"Yes, I suppose it is."

"What happened, Mr. St. Ives?"

"Nothing happened. They just didn't show up."

"They?"

"I suppose it's a they."

"This was only to test your reliability then?"

"I don't know," I said. "Maybe they spotted you flouncing around in the Cadillac. Neither you nor it is exactly inconspicuous."

"Do you mean that they were here at the motel?"

"I didn't say that. I don't know where they are. They just called me on the phone and told me the deal was off."

"But they made another rendezvous, of course."

There was nothing for me to say to that and Mbwato seemed to realize it. He reached over and patted me on the knee with his left hand, which was not much larger than a ping-pong paddle. "Let me assure you, Mr. St. Ives, that if we had been successful in securing the shield this evening, we would have also made certain that you would have retained the funds that are in your trust."

"You don't know how relieved I am."

He gave me the smile then, the one that promised to glow for a thousand hours. "There may come a time when you will welcome our interest and even our participation."

"I doubt that," I said.

The smile had vanished. Mbwato was serious now, even grave. "Don't be too certain, Mr. St. Ives," he

129

said in a deep, melancholy voice that seemed to rumble up from some forgotten sepulcher.

"I'm not certain about anything."

That seemed to cheer him up a little. He smiled again and said, "By the way, I took the liberty of ordering a wreath for the funeral of Mr. Frank Spellacy. Anonymously, of course. I hope you approve."

"I don't know any Frank Spellacy."

"That's right. You saw him only once. And even then, I believe, he was already quite dead."

I opened the door to the Cadillac. "You do keep busy, don't you?" I said to Mbwato.

He smiled again. "Yes, Mr. St. Ives. We do keep busy because we have so little time. So very little time."

13

It had been a long, fretful drive back to Manhattan, made doubly grating by a spectacular five-car pile-up that had killed two persons and slowed three miles of New York-bound traffic to a creep. By the time I drove into the Avis garage I was irritable; by the time I arrived at the Adelphi by cab, toting the fifty-eight pounds of money, I was testy; and when I spotted Lieutenant Kenneth Ogden of vice slumped comfortably in one of the chairs in the lobby, looking as if he had just taken squatter's rights, I suffered a severe internal implosion which, everything considered, was kept under pretty fair control. I could have stamped my foot.

Ogden slowly got out of his chair when I came in and permitted me another long examination of his false teeth. "No luck, huh?" He seemed happy about it.

"No."

"Just feeling you out," he said. "They do that sometimes."

"I know."

"It's in there?" he said, gesturing toward the suit-case.

"It's in there," I said.

Ogden licked his lips and I tried to remember where I had last seen that look. It's an unusual look; really quite rare. The eyes narrow, the lips grow wet and move a little, there's sometimes a faint smile plus an air of total concentration and an obliviousness to everything but the satiation soon to come. I remembered then: it was a fat man in a cafeteria. He had weighed a little more than three hundred pounds and he had had that same look when he sat down to an assortment of dishes that would have stuffed four persons with ordinary appetites. With the fat man it had been food; with Ogden it was money. With both it was greed.

"What're you going to do with it?" he said.

"The hotel's got a safe."

"I saw it. You could open it with a corkscrew."

"There's somebody on duty all night."

Ogden snorted, his eyes still fixed on the suitcase, which was growing heavy. I switched it to my left hand. "Hell, he must be seventy-five and besides, he sleeps all night."

"Would you like to keep it for me overnight?"

"Well, we could for Christ's sake at least take it down to the precinct station. It'd be safe there."

I walked over to the hotel desk. Ogden followed. "You remember the Baxter kidnaping out in Omaha about fifteen years ago?" I said.

He looked at me and a sour, suspicious look crept across his face. "Look, St. Ives—"

"Baxter was kidnaped, you remember, and held for $200,000 ransom." The room clerk appeared at the desk, an aged, frail man whom I knew only as Charlie.

"Evening, Mr. St. Ives."

"Hello, Charlie. Any messages?"

He glanced at my box. I could have done it just as

easily, but I always asked him because he liked to be asked and at seventy-five there aren't many things that anyone will ask you for. "Not a thing," he said.

"Will you put this in the safe?" I said, and swung the suitcase up on the counter. He tried to pick it up with one hand, failed, and barely managed to get it off the counter with two. I watched him unlock the safe and store the suitcase inside. Ogden was right. It looked as if it could be opened with a corkscrew. Or a hairpin. But it was safer than my bathtub. I turned to Ogden, who was also watching and who looked as if all the dreams that he'd ever had in his life were being locked away, out of sight forever.

"So when Baxter was kidnaped," I said.

"Who?" Ogden said.

"Baxter. The man out in Omaha."

"Oh. Yeah." He didn't seem very interested.

"When Baxter was kidnaped they asked two hundred thousand and the family agreed to pay. They turned the money over to a cop, a lieutenant of detectives, as I recall, who was supposed to make the money drop, pick up some instructions about where he'd find Baxter, and then fetch him back to his hearth and home. Well, this lieutenant dropped off the money okay and he picked up the directions about where he could find Baxter. But he was the ambitious type, so he staked out the money drop until the kidnapers showed up. He tried to take them, and there was a gun fight. According to the lieutenant there were three of them and he killed two. The other one, again according to the lieutenant, got away with the ransom money. About an hour after he was supposed to be there, the lieutenant finally drove up to the deserted farmhouse where Baxter was held. He was about an hour too late. Baxter had choked to death on the gag that the kidnapers had placed in his mouth. At least that's what the autopsy said."

Ogden gave me one of his mean looks, the one that he probably used on whores and pimps and the sad-faced, middle-aged men who hung around the toilet at the YMCA. It was a look in which all the lines in the face seem to run downward. "You trying to say something, St. Ives?"

"I'm telling a story."

"Has it got a point?"

"I think so; it might even have a moral. So there was the Baxter family, not only out $200,000 but minus its bread-winner as well. They never caught the third kidnaper; they never recovered any of the money; and the lieutenant of detectives resigned two months later and retired to Hawaii at age thirty-eight."

Ogden grunted. "I remember it all right. The cop got a lot of guff about if there really was a third man who took off with the ransom. And there was even some who thought that he might have helped the guy —what's his name, Baxter—that he might have helped him to choke to death a little. If he was gagged real good, and tied up real good, all the cop would have to do is hold his nose for five minutes or so."

"But it was convenient, wasn't it?" I said. "With Baxter dead, no one could ever be sure—except the lieutenant, of course—about whether there really was a third man."

"You said it had a moral. I don't see any moral."

"How about: the wise man resists temptation but for a moment; the dull man for an hour, and the fool forever?" Another none-too-pithy aphorism. Perhaps I could soon start talking in parables.

"Did you make that up?" Ogden said.

"I think so."

"What is it, some kind of a crack?"

"Not really."

"That story about the Omaha kidnaping was."

"All right."

We had walked over to the elevators and I punched the up button. There was no one else in the lobby except Charlie behind the desk. The night bellhop was hiding somewhere and the cigar counter, out of stamps again, no doubt, had closed promptly at its regular hour of six.

"You going up?" Ogden asked.

"I thought I might; you want to tuck me in?"

"No, I just wanted to make sure you got home safe and sound."

"And you took part of your day off to do it."

"That's right," he said, "I did. You know what else I did today on my day off?"

"What?"

"I went to a funeral. Frank Spellacy's. You knew Frank." It wasn't a question the way he asked it.

"No. I didn't know Frank."

"Funny. I thought you did. I thought you might have written him up in your column. He was a kind of character, always operating on the edge. Funny how he died."

"How?"

"Somebody stuck a knife in his throat and he bled to death all over his desk and rug. He had an office in the Nickerson Building over on Park Avenue. He was hustling lots out in the desert somewhere. That's what he did mostly, but he had a sideline. You know what it was?"

"No," I said, wishing that the elevator would come so that I could vanish into it.

"He ran a reference bureau. You know, if somebody wanted something done then Frank could put them in touch with who could do it. Or if somebody wanted to check out somebody, and they didn't want to bother with the Better Business Bureau, why they'd call up Frank and he'd find out for them. A lot of bookies used him."

"Sounds like a character," I said, and punched the elevator button again, hard.

"He had a nice funeral. Over in Queens. Lots of friends. And you say you didn't know him?"

"No. I didn't know him."

135

"That's funny."

"What?"

"He knew you. He had a whole file on you, homicide says. A new one."

"I'm in a funny business. Maybe that's why he had a file."

"Maybe. But the homicide boys also found something on his calendar—you know, the appointment book that he kept on his desk."

"What?"

"Just your name with four o'clock beside it on the day he died. Yesterday. But homicide's not much interested; old Frank had been long dead by four o'clock as near as the medical report could figure, which, of course, isn't too accurate."

I'd had enough. "What do you want, Ogden? Spell it out."

He glanced around the lobby, leaned toward me, and tapped a manicured forefinger against my lapel. I don't like to be tapped. "I want in."

"There's no room."

"Make it."

"Not a chance."

"Two hundred and fifty thousand's a lot of money."

"I don't like jails."

"No jails. You make the switch, the money for the shield. The museum's happy. But you take me along to make another switch. The money into our pockets, an even split, and who's to squawk?"

"The thieves. They wouldn't like it at all."

"Who they gonna complain to?"

"Christ, they could write a letter to the editor and even if it weren't published, it would be turned over to the cops who'd be swarming around for the next ten years."

The greed was back on Ogden's face. His wet lips moved, making little smacking noises, and his eyes squinted at me as if I gave off some blinding but irresistible glow. "The thieves don't have to be around after it's over," he said, running his words together. "That's the beauty of it. They don't have to be around to complain."

I could only stare at him, at the wet lips and the squinted eyes and the haunched, almost supplicating stance. "I believe you'd do it," I said. "Goddamn, I believe you'd do it."

He looked around the lobby once more. It was an almost furtive glance. "I'm fifty-three years old, St. Ives, and I want in on this. I'm gonna retire in a couple of years. A hundred and twenty-five grand would make it livable."

"Get it from your whores, Ogden. Not from me."

"I'm cutting myself in."

"No, I don't think so."

"I've got a kicker."

"I thought you might."

"You see, St. Ives," he said in a hoarse whisper after conning the lobby again. "I know who the thieves are."

It was his exit line and he had been working up to it all evening. He grinned at me with all those terrible teeth, nodded a couple of times, happily, I thought, turned and strode across the faded lobby, through the door, and out into the summer night.

"The elevator, Mr. St. Ives," Charlie called from the desk. "It ain't working."

14

It was raining when I awakened at seven the next morning, a hard stinging rain whose drops committed mass suicide against my ninth-floor window where I stood and watched while the water boiled on the two-burner stove for instant coffee. Armed with the coffee and the day's first cigarette, I picked up the phone and called Eastern Airlines, which answered on the fourteenth ring. All flights to Washington had been canceled. It was raining hard in Washington too. It was probably raining all over the world.

That left the bus or the train. I called the Pennsylvania Central Railroad and the man who answered on the twenty-second ring was indifferent about whether I ever got to Washington, or it may have been that he was preoccupied with what kind of cake his great-great-grandaughter would serve when he got home that night to celebrate his ninety-second birthday. He finally admitted, after some coaxing, that there was a train leaving for Washington at eight that morning and if I were nice, he might even sell me a ticket.

I called down to the desk and got Eddie, the day bellhop. "It's worth two bucks if you've got a cab waiting for me when I get downstairs in ten minutes," I said.

"Jesus, Mr. St. Ives, I'll get all wet."

I sighed. "Three bucks."

"Okay. Three bucks. By the way, that horse you picked the other day."

"What about it?"

"It didn't win."

"Thanks."

"Don't mention it. You want to get down on something today?"

"No time."

"You want I should pick one for you?"

"The cab, Eddie."

I dressed in four minutes, packed a shirt, underwear, socks, and toilet articles into an overnight bag in two minutes, added a fifth of Scotch, waited for the miraculously repaired elevator for a minute, and was in the lobby at the desk asking for the suitcase nine minutes after I had talked to Eddie. I was also unshaved, unwashed, and unhappy.

The bellhop had somehow managed to find a cab. "I got all wet," he said as I handed him three dollars. It was as close to thank you as he ever got. The cab driver grunted when I told him where I wanted to go, then mumbled to himself all the way to Penn Station. It took fifteen minutes to go the mile which, on a rainy morning in Manhattan, might have broken some kind of speed record. At seven-forty I queued up at the ticket counter behind a woman who wanted to take a train to Cutbank, Montana. She didn't want to go today, and she didn't know whether she would leave next week or the week after, because she wasn't sure when her daughter's baby was due, but she thought that she'd get all the information now and decide later, after she heard from her daughter. The man behind the counter became interested in her story and they gossiped about babies for a while and then he thumbed through some thick black books which told him whether a train went through Cutbank. After he figured out her route and she wrote it down they chatted some more, this time about the weather. I didn't think that he was the same man whom I'd talked to over the phone because he wasn't much over seventy-five.

When the Montana-bound woman finally left, the man behind the counter looked at me suspiciously, as if I wanted to buy a ticket or make him an indecent proposition. I think he would have preferred the proposition.

"Washington, a parlor seat."

"Don't know if I got one left," he said, glancing up at the clock and then over at his rack of tickets. "You're a little late, you know."

"It's all my fault."

"Parlor car, huh. That costs more'n coach."

"I know."

"You still want it?"

"I still want it," I said, not even yelling.

"Only got one left."

"I wouldn't want to run you short."

"Coach'd only cost you $10.75. Parlor cost you $19.90. That's a lot of money."

"I just came into an inheritance."

"Huh," he said, and slid the ticket over to me as I handed him a twenty-dollar bill. "Look after the pennies, I say, and the dollars will take care of themselves."

"You think that up all by yourself?" I said as he slid my dime to me.

"Been saying it all my life." He looked at the clock again. It was three minutes until eight. "If you hurry," he said comfortably, "you might still make it."

I hurried, the fifty-eight-pound suitcase banging against my right knee. There was really no need. The train was ten minutes late in pulling out.

The last train ride I took was the Trans-Europ-Express from Cologne to Paris. The food had been good, the service excellent, the ride fast, and the track smooth. The Pennsylvania Central Railroad offered none of these. I had paid $8.15 extra for the privilege of sitting in a chair that swung 360° so that I'd miss none of the megalopolitan mess that was the eastern seaboard of the United States. There were some factories to look at, some junk yards, several vistas of rather interesting slums, and one cow.

I'm not sure when it was that American railroads went to the bad. Some claim that it started as far back as the twenties, but it was probably just after World War II, when they began building super-highways and you could buy a car again and an airplane ride was no longer much of an adventure. It must have been a gradual decline. The coaches and the Pullmans that wore out were junked and not replaced. The crack train became a joke. The help got old and died and nobody much wanted to work for the railroads anymore. Then suddenly, sometime in the mid-sixties, the country awakened to learn that its skies and highways were choked while its rails were empty. At least of passenger service. Between Washington and New York they finally got one new high-speed Metroliner running, but only once a day, and it was supposed to make the 227-mile trip in two hours and fifty-nine minutes—an hour faster than the Greyhound bus. Someday they may even run it all the way up to Boston.

Meanwhile, in car or bus, you could creep along highways that were built for the traffic of the early fifties or go by planes that stacked up for hours over airports that turned obsolete as soon as they were completed.

Many of the good ones were gone, I thought. The Commodore Vanderbilt and the 20th Century Limited, for instance. Even the Wabash Cannonball. Yet elsewhere in the world trains were still running, most of them on time. You could go from Tokyo to Osaka, 320 miles, in three hours and ten minutes on the New Tokaido Line. The Blue Train still ran luxuriously from Johannesburg to Capetown, and on the Rheingold you could go from Amsterdam to Geneva, 657 miles, in a little more than eleven hours and dictate to a secretary who spoke four languages while you stared out the window at the castles on the Rhine. I doubted that I could even get a decent cup of coffee on the Penn Central.

At one o'clock we pulled into Washington's rococo Union Station, almost an hour late. It was still raining hard and I had to wait fifteen minutes for a cab. By the time I got to the Madison and into my room, it was a quarter to two. I called down for a large breakfast and then went into the bathroom to get rid of my beard and the grubbiness of the train.

After breakfast, I called Lieutenant Demeter. "Nice of you to check in," he said. "How's the bag-man business?"

"They called a fake switch in a motel about halfway across New Jersey to see how well I follow instructions."

"But they didn't show."

"No."

"Maybe you'd better drop around and tell me about it."

"I can't," I said. "I was supposed to check in here at twelve-thirty, but the planes aren't flying and I had to take a train so I was late. They're supposed to call me here."

"Have you got the money with you?" Demeter said.

"Yes."

"Where?"

"Here. In my room."

Demeter exploded. "For Christ sake, St. Ives, get it into the hotel safe. Maybe it's different in New York. Maybe the people up there are all beautiful and gentle and fond of flowers, but I wouldn't walk across the street in this town with more than forty bucks cash in my pocket." He seemed to turn his head away from the phone. "He's got the money in his room, for Christ sake." He must have been talking to Sergeant Fastnaught.

"I'd planned to put it in the safe."

"Quit planning and do it. Where you staying, the Madison again?"

"Yes."

"What's your room number?"

I told him.

"We'll be there in half an hour."

With the money safely stored in the Madison's vault, I went back up to my room and stood by the window and watched it rain some more. Twenty minutes later there was a bump at the door; not a knock, but a bump that was followed by a dry, scratching sound as if someone were trying to peel off the paint. I moved to the door and opened it. It was Ogden and his face was screwed up into a wrinkle of pain as the tears ran down his cheeks that had all the color of old paste.

"Lemme in," he said. "Lemme in."

I let him in, and he stumbled. He was wearing a tan raincoat and he pressed it tight against his belly with both hands, but even the raincoat didn't stop the blood from seeping through his fingers.

"On the bed," I said, and grabbed his arm and helped him over to it. He wouldn't lie down. He sat there on the edge of the bed and held his stomach.

"Oh, God, I hurt! Get a doctor, get me a doctor."

I picked up the phone and dialed the operator. "Send a doctor up to 429," I said. "A man has been injured."

She didn't argue or ask questions. "I'll call the emergency ambulance."

"Do something," I snapped.

Ogden had fallen over on the bed, his head rested on the pillow, his feet were still on the floor, and his hands still clutched the widening red stain on his raincoat.

"In the lobby," he muttered. "He used the goddamn knife right in the lobby."

"Who?"

"Both of them were there. That bitch giggled when he did it." Ogden groaned and the groan grew into a scream. "Why do I have to suffer so?" he moaned, but I couldn't think of an answer.

"Who was in the lobby, Ogden?" I said.

"Get me a doctor. Get me a goddamn doctor."

"He's on his way. Who was in the lobby?"

"You got the money?" he said, and struggled to get up. "You got the money? Lemme see it. Lemme see the money."

"It's not here; it's in the vault. Who stabbed you, Ogden?"

"I saw 'em on the train and then they came here and the bitch giggled when he did it."

"Who, goddamnit?" I said.

"That pimp, Freddie. That pimp and his whore."

"Freddie, who?"

Freddie something he started to say but the blood bubbled out of his mouth, and then there was a big gush of it that went all over the pillow, and Lieutenant Kenneth Ogden of the New York Police Department's vice squad lay still on the bed, very still and dead.

The phone rang and I picked it up. "We're downstairs and on our way up," Demeter said.

"You're too late," I said, and hung up.

15

The assistant manager of the Madison looked as if he wished that I would go to another hotel, preferably in another town. After I had told my story to three plainclothes detectives from the homicide squad who had been summoned by Lieutenant Demeter, I told it again. And then, just to make sure that I'd left nothing out, I told it a third time. When one of the homicide detectives asked for a fourth rendition, I turned to Demeter, who leaned against the door and stared at the body of his former FBI Academy classmate, Lieutenant Kenneth Ogden of the New York Police Department. Fastnaught was at the window looking at the rain.

"The fourth time won't be any different from the third or the second or the first," I said.

Demeter didn't look at me; he kept on staring at the body on the bed. "Just tell it, St. Ives. Just tell what happened."

So I told the three homicide detectives how Ogden

had died on the bed in my room. One of the detectives was a weary fifty, a stocky man with spiky inchlong gray hair that formed a kind of dull halo around his face. It was the face of a disappointed listener who had grown tired of waiting for punch lines that never came.

"Start with last night this time, Mr. St. Ives," he said. "When Ogden approached you in your hotel in New York."

After I told it for the fourth time they removed the body of Ogden on a wheeled stretcher. Technicians and blue coats had been in and out of the room, poking into the medicine cabinet, counting my socks in the bureau, and making themselves generally useful. Somebody took some pictures of Ogden's body, but no one bothered about fingerprints. The assistant manager had been in and out twice, looking mortified the first time and despondent the second. The third time he showed up while they were wheeling the body out and this time he looked alarmed. "Down the service elevator, please, down the service elevator," he said, turning to Demeter. "Can't you tell them to take it down the service elevator?"

"We're parked out front," one of the ambulance attendants said.

"The service elevator," Demeter said, and I thought the assistant manager might kiss his hand.

"It's awful," the assistant manager said to no one in particular. "It's just God-awful."

"Tell you what you do," Demeter said.

"Yes, yes," the assistant manager said. "What? What?" He was very nervous and he ran a thin pale hand through his ample black hair, which looked as if it had been cut by a razor, teased, and sprayed.

"Get him another room," Demeter said, and jerked a thumb at me.

"He's going to stay?" and there was shock and disapproval and even a touch of horror in the question. "You're not taking him with you?"

"No, he's not coming with us. He likes it here, don't you, St. Ives?"

"Because it's so homey," I said.

The assistant manager shook his head and this time he registered despair. He had an extremely mobile face. "I'll send a man up with a key," he said, and left.

Demeter turned to the detective with the spiky gray hair. "You got what you need from St. Ives?" he said.

"Such as it is."

"I like the part where Ogden wanted in on the $250,000," Demeter said.

"They're going to like that up in New York, too," the homicide detective said. "Oh, they're going to like it all just real fine. What they're really going to like though is Ogden's wanting to zing the thieves after he got the money and the shield. They're going to eat that right up." He got up from the chair he'd been sitting in, walked over to me, and stood there for a few moments. "Anything else you'd like to add, Mr. St. Ives?"

"Nothing," I said.

"We're going to need a formal statement from you."

"All right," I said. "When?"

"Tomorrow."

"When?"

"Oh, say ten o'clock? Or is that too early for you?"

"That's fine."

"Uh-huh," he said, and turned to Demeter. "You knew Ogden, you say?"

"I knew him," Demeter said, and his tone was flat and careful.

"Well?"

"We went through the FBI Academy together, back in the fifties."

"What do you think?"

"Nothing," Demeter said. "I think absolutely nothing."

"That's a big help," the homicide detective said. "If you get around to thinking something, let me know."

He made a brusque wave with his hand at the other two homicide detectives who were younger and taller and not quite so tired-looking. "Come on," he said, "let's go down to the lobby and find out how many eyewitnesses we got." He turned to Demeter once again. "You know how many we're going to have?"

"How many?"

"Less than one. Zero." He moved to the door, opened it, and let the two other detectives through. Then he turned and looked at the bed with its blood-soaked pillows and spread. "God, the paperwork," he said. "You know something?" he said to Demeter.

"What?"

"A cop should get killed in his own home town."

A bellhop arrived shortly after the homicide detectives left, ogled the blood, picked up my overnight bag which I had repacked, and led Demeter, Fastnaught, and me past the uniformed cop stationed outside the door, down the hall, into the elevator, up two floors and into another room. "Lot of blood," he said as he unlocked the door. No one seemed to want to contradict him so he stood around until I remembered to give him a tip. Fastnaught walked over to the window and resumed his inspection of the rain. Demeter selected a chair and eased himself into it as if the dampness made his joints stiff. I opened the overnight case and took out the bottle of Scotch.

"You want a drink?" I said.

"Water," Fastnaught said.

"Just water or Scotch and water?"

"Scotch and water."

"Lieutenant?"

"Sure," he said. "Why not?"

I mixed three drinks and handed them around. Fastnaught turned from the window and rested his rear on the sill. Demeter produced one of his cigars and ritualistically lighted it. I sank into an armchair opposite Demeter.

"Well, what do you think, Sergeant Fastnaught?" Demeter said.

Fastnaught took a swallow of his drink before answering. "I think," he said slowly, "that we got ourselves a whole new ball game."

"What makes you say that, Sergeant Fastnaught?" Demeter said, and wiped some of his drink from his Ronald Colman mustache.

"Your friend Ogden," Fastnaught said.

"My friend Ogden," Demeter said softly. "I wonder what happened to my friend Ogden. When I first met him more than fifteen years ago all he wanted to do was show you pictures of his baby daughter. He was enthused about the whole thing then, a hell of a lot more than I was. I wonder how he felt the first time he got hold of some of that easy money. When you're on the vice squad it's always floating around. Just stick out your hand and somebody will lay a couple of hundred in it. And around Christmas, I suppose, with a wife and a baby daughter, a couple of hundred can make a lot of difference. Maybe it was around Christmas that my friend Ogden stuck his hand out for the first time. What do you think, St. Ives?"

"He was a crook," I said. "He was a crook who for a slice of $250,000 wouldn't mind becoming a murderer."

"Is that a moral judgment, St. Ives?"

"It's only what he told me he was."

"And were you shocked, maybe a little surprised?"

"No," I said. "Not particularly."

"Why not, St. Ives? Didn't you have even a bit of what the editorials call 'moral indignation' or outraged sensibility? Why didn't you report him? Why didn't you go down and see his superior and say, 'By the way, this Ogden that works for you. I'm afraid he's something of a wrong one, a shade dishonest, you might say.'"

I found a cigarette and lit it. "How much do you pay for your suits, Lieutenant?"

"Seventy-five tops, and that's the one I wear to Mass."

"How about you, Sergeant Fastnaught?"

He smiled a little. "I paid one twenty-five once, but then I'm not married."

"Ogden paid at least $300 for his suits. He drove a Lincoln Continental. His wife had a Buick. He played table-stakes poker and could drop $500 without a blink. He lived in a co-op apartment that cost God knows how much, but not less than $80,000 and that doesn't include maintenance. I knew this and I didn't see Ogden but maybe a dozen times a year when we played poker. Now if I knew this, then the people he worked for knew it, so why should I play Morally Outraged Citizen? And just who the hell do I tell about it? His superior, you say. For all I know his superior had cut himself in for twenty-five percent."

"Suppose," Demeter said, and looked up at the ceiling, "suppose Fastnaught here and me made you a proposition, maybe something like you say Ogden made you?"

"He made it," I said.

"Suppose we made it then. Would you be surprised?"

"I'd be surprised."

"Why? Because we wear cheap suits?"

"No."

Demeter leaned forward in his chair and stared at me with his beany eyes. "You got something built into your head, St. Ives? Some kind of a gauge that tells you this cop's honest and this one's a crook? You got something like that?"

"No."

"Then how about me and Fastnaught? How can you tell we're honest?"

"Because I don't know any differently."

"And you'd be surprised if we made you a proposition?"

"I've already said that."

150

Demeter finished his drink and placed it on a table beside his chair. I didn't ask him whether he wanted another one. He tapped off an inch of cigar ash into a tray, looked at Fastnaught, who nodded, and then leaned back comfortably in the chair.

"Fastnaught and me," he said, "are going to make you a proposition. We talked about it on the way over here, even before we knew that Ogden was mixed up in the deal. Now we'd like to get your considered opinion. You say that Ogden knew who the thieves were?"

"He said he did."

"And you figure they killed him because he knew?"

"Probably."

Demeter puffed on his cigar. "Now that he's dead, you think they'll go ahead with the switch?"

"How should I know?"

"I think they will," Demeter said. "What do you think, Fastnaught?"

"Another dead one won't bother them," Fastnaught said.

"You're probably right," Demeter said. "How many does that make now?" He stuck the cigar in his mouth and started counting on his left hand. "There's Sackett, the spade guard, that's one. Ogden makes two. And there was this guy, Frank Spellacy, up in New York. You forgot to mention him to the homicide boys, St. Ives."

"So did you," I said.

"Well, we're not sure about him."

"Who told you? Ogden?"

"No. Not Ogden. Ogden's not the only cop I know in New York."

"He even knows a couple of honest ones," Fastnaught said.

"Let's just say that we found out that you had an appointment with Frank Spellacy the day he got killed and that Ogden put in a word or two for you."

"All right," I said.

Demeter was counting on his left hand again. "Now

how many's that? The guard, Ogden, and Spellacy. That's three. Any more, Fastnaught?"

"One more," Fastnaught said from his seat at the window. "George Wingo."

"That's right, George Wingo. Mrs. Wingo's husband. But you knew about him, didn't you, St. Ives? I mean you knew he was a junkie?"

"I knew," I said.

"The Coroner's Office said you were asking, and that you had some assistant U.S. Attorney General call up and find out for you."

"You get around," I said.

"Just routine police work. Even the Coroner's Office thought it was something of a coincidence when Fastnaught here asks for the autopsy report one day and the assistant attorney general asks for it the next. So the guy at the Coroner's Office calls us, we call the assistant attorney general, and he says he did it as a favor for that lawyer of yours ... what's his name?"

"Myron Greene," Fastnaught said.

"Greene," Demeter said. "So what'd you think when you found out that both Sackett, the guard, and Mr. Wingo were junkies?"

"Nothing," I said.

"Bullshit," Fastnaught said.

"Come on, Fastnaught," Demeter said. "Maybe St. Ives hasn't got a keen deductive mind like yours. You know what Fastnaught thought?"

I sighed. "That Wingo got the guard hooked and then talked him into being the inside man when the shield was stolen. That's what a five-year-old would think anyway. At least what my five-year-old would think, but then he's got a high IQ."

"Probably got it from his daddy," Demeter said. "So the way Fastnaught figures it is that Wingo is desperate for a wad of money that'll keep him in smack. Because he's something of an art expert he decides to steal the shield and then sell it back to the museum. But he needs help; he needs not only the inside man but the outside thieves. Now where's he going to find them?"

"Spellacy," I said.

"You'd be a credit to the force, St. Ives. How'd you figure that?"

"When I was in Spellacy's office, he wrote Wingo's name on a pad. It was the last thing he ever wrote."

"And you didn't tell anyone?"

"No."

"You could have saved us a lot of trouble," Fastnaught said. "A hell of a lot of trouble."

"You sure could have," Demeter said. "We had to go see Mrs. Wingo last night and tell her what we thought. She didn't like it; she didn't like it worth a damn. But then she let us go through her husband's papers and we ran across some correspondence between him and Spellacy."

"What kind of correspondence?" I said.

"About some stocks that Wingo had bought through Spellacy maybe six or seven years ago when he was still in New York. It seems Spellacy sold Wingo short on some stocks that were supposed to go down. They went up instead. Spellacy owed Wingo quite a hunk of money. So we called New York about Spellacy. It was the only thing we had and they told us that Spellacy had just been done in. They also gave us a rundown on him and he seemed to be the kind of a guy who might have lined up a couple of thieves for Wingo."

"And a go-between," I said. "He checked me out for Wingo."

"And you didn't bother to tell anyone about that either," Fastnaught said. "You're not much of a gossip, are you, St. Ives?"

"Well, what do you expect from a high-priced go-between, Fastnaught?" Demeter said. "You expect him to go around blabbing everything he knows to cops who're probably crooked even if they don't wear three-hundred-dollar suits?"

"I suppose you're right," Fastnaught said. "I shouldn't expect that."

I got up and mixed myself another drink. I didn't ask either of them if they wanted one. "Now what?"

"You want to hear our theory?"

"I thought I'd just heard it," I said. "Wingo masterminded the theft of the shield to keep himself in heroin. He got himself an inside man by getting the guard hooked. Then he got in touch with Spellacy, who set him up with a couple of thieves, the man and the woman who've been calling me on the phone. When everything was planned, the pair got greedy, gave Wingo an overdose of heroin, and then rolled him down an embankment in his car. They took over then and when the guard had done his job, they blew his head off. Spellacy figures most of it out and threatens to talk unless he gets a bigger cut so they shove a knife into him. They did the same thing to Ogden an hour or so ago down in the lobby. I don't know how Ogden found out who they were, if he really did, but then I don't really care."

"What do you mean, you don't care, St. Ives?" Demeter said in a quiet voice.

"Just what I said. There're too many dead bodies." I got up and walked over to the far wall and examined a print of some medieval gateway. "I'm bowing out," I said. "Quitting."

"He's getting carefully cautious again, Lieutenant," Fastnaught said.

"Uh-huh," Demeter said. "So it seems."

"You can find someone else," I said. "Someone who might enjoy the risk."

"Sit down, St. Ives," Demeter said, and his voice sounded like thick ice cracking. "Sit down and I'll tell you why you goddamn sure as hell aren't quitting."

16

Sergeant Fastnaught left his seat at the window and moved over to the door. He leaned against it as though it were the most comfortable spot in the room. An itch seemed to develop between his shoulder blades because he rubbed his back against the molding of the door without shifting his gaze from me. Demeter leaned forward in the chair, his big, tightly curled head thrust forward, his red lips slightly parted as he breathed through his mouth. The cigar burned unnoticed in his right hand.

"What you'd really like me to do is put the Scotch in my bag and try to go through that door," I said. "That's really what you'd like."

"Get off it, St. Ives," Fastnaught said.

Demeter looked at him. "Well, now, Sergeant Fastnaught, what do you expect him to think? I've just told him that he's not going to quit and there you are at the door, looking for all the world like you'd like to bust him in the mouth if he tried to go through it. St.

Ives has got a point and we ought to respect it. After all the talk about police brutality, what do you expect him to think?"

"Sorry," Fastnaught said in a voice that was a couple of blocks away from being contrite. "I forgot about the role assigned to us by society. Of course, busting him in the mouth could help us pad out our scrapbooks. Paste in some clippings with headlines like 'Police Pummel New York Go-Between in Hotel' or even 'Cops Clobber New York Man in Posh Hotel.'"

Demeter nodded gravely. "You've got a flair, Sergeant Fastnaught. I'd say you've got almost a real genius for public relations. Don't you agree, St. Ives?"

"He's a wonder," I said.

"Now then," Demeter said, leaning back comfortably in the chair and drawing on his cigar. "I was going to tell you why you're not going to back out, wasn't I?"

"You did mention that, but maybe I'd better go first. Maybe I'd better tell you why I *am* going to back out."

Demeter waved his cigar at me. "The floor is yours."

"If your mathematics are right, four people have been killed over this shield. The reason that they were killed is that they either knew or had a pretty good idea who stole it. So there's a very good chance that anybody who'd shove a knife into a New York cop in the lobby of the Madison Hotel would be less than queasy about getting permanently rid of a go-between about three o'clock in the morning on some lonely road in Virginia or Maryland. But even if they come up with a safe switch, one that involves no contact, I'm still the loose end, the one they'd wake up at five o'clock in the morning and start worrying about, wondering if they'd somehow made a slip and that I just might be able to identify them. Now that's only a slight chance, maybe a ten-to-one shot, but it's more than I'm willing to take for twenty-five thousand or even fifty thousand. I'm sure you follow me."

"Perfectly," Demeter said.

"Then that's it; I'm out."

"No," Demeter said. "You're not."

"Don't push it," I said.

Demeter got out of his chair and walked over to the window. "Washington's a funny town," he said. "It's not like New York or Chicago or even Philadelphia. When you get right down to it, a handful of congressmen run this town and if anybody's got a hold on those congressmen, then he's got a pretty good grip on Washington, too. You follow me, St. Ives?"

"I follow you."

"You notice how polite the homicide boys were? Not many questions, not much excitement, just kind of a quiet routine even though a cop was killed and an out-of-town cop at that."

"I noticed."

"It'll probably be about two paragraphs back with the leg-sore ads. No more. You see, St. Ives, the word's come down. They want that shield back without any fuss. Now you're going to ask where'd it come down from and I can't answer that because I don't know, but if I was to guess I'd say it came down from 1600 Pennsylvania Avenue, drifted up to Capitol Hill, and sort of trickled down to Fastnaught and me. We got the riot act read to us the other day—day before yesterday, wasn't it, Fastnaught?"

"Day before yesterday," Fastnaught said.

"They used the carrot and the stick on us. They told about all the nice things that were going to happen to us if we got the shield back and then they told us about all the not-so-nice things that were going to happen if we didn't. They weren't bothered that some people were dead because of a hunk of brass. That didn't worry them one bit. All they want is the shield back and they gave us carte blanche—that's the right expression, isn't it? So Fastnaught here speaks up and says, 'What happens if the go-between gets cold feet and wants to back out?' Well, they just looked at us for a long time and then one of them said, 'I trust you've heard of harassment, Lieutenant Demeter?' So I said yes, I'd heard of it. And then they just looked at us some more."

"Being harassed is better than being dead," I said.

Demeter turned from the window and shook his head, a little sadly, I thought. "You're not going to be dead, St. Ives. Not if Fastnaught and I can help it. Let me tell you something. My whole future's riding on you. Fastnaught's younger; he could do something else, but I'm past forty-five and that's too old to start all over again. Now when they say harassment, they mean it. They'll drag you through courts on income tax. You'll spend every dime you've got on lawyers. And if you go on living in New York—or anyplace else—they'll send some buttons after you at three o'clock in the morning with a warrant for your arrest for jaywalking or spitting on the sidewalk. Your life won't be worth living. I don't say I like the idea, but there's lots of things in this country I don't like."

"It's just your job," I said.

"That's right, St. Ives, it's just my job and some days I don't have to like that either."

It was still raining and for what seemed to be a long time the rain on the window was the only sound in the room. Demeter went back to his chair; Fastnaught maintained his vigilance at the other door, and I crossed to the window and stared down at Fifteenth Street and the shiny tops of wet cars. The pressure could have come, as Demeter said, from the White House, from one of those faceless aides who'd been chivvied by someone at State. Or it could have come from a senator or a matched pair of congressmen who owed their re-election to someone, someone who wanted the shield back and not too many questions asked. But the pressure was there all right, strong enough to bend a couple of tough cops and leave a sour taste in their mouths. And the threat of harassment was real, too. I'd seen harassment before, a couple of times, and one had wound up in a sanitarium and the other had fled to Italy, which he didn't much like but which he liked better than what he'd gone through in New York for eighteen months before his nerves shattered.

I turned from the window and looked at Demeter, who was staring at the floor. "You win," I said.

"Some prize," Demeter said to the rug on the floor. "I win a go-between. A brass go-between."

The phone finally rang at three-thirty. Fastnaught was stretched out on one of the twin beds. Demeter was still in his chair reading a newspaper that I'd sent down for. The voice on the phone was the man again and he still had a mouthful of wet cotton.

"Do you know Washington?" the voice asked.

"No."

"There's a golf driving range in the northwest section." He gave me the address. "Do you have that?"

"Yes."

"Be there at exactly ten-fifteen tonight. Have the money in a suitcase in the back seat of a four-door sedan. Park your car, but don't get out of it. At exactly ten-twenty the back door will be opened. Don't look around. I mean it. Don't look around. The shield will be put in your back seat. Wait five minutes and then you can do whatever you want to do. Have you got all that?"

"I've got it."

The phone went dead and I hung up. Fastnaught was sitting up on the bed; Demeter had put his paper on the floor. Both of them were looking at me.

"Tonight at ten-fifteen," I said. Then I told them what the cottony voice had told me.

"Sort of a public place, isn't it?" Demeter said.

"Not if it's still raining," I said.

Fastnaught went to the window and peered out. "It's stopped," he said. "Looks like it might clear up."

159

Demeter rose and stretched. "Ten-fifteen tonight, huh?" he said. "How's your golf game, Fastnaught?"

"Lousy."

"Maybe you'll get a chance to improve it tonight, but right now we've got some work to do."

"You're not leaving?" I said.

"Sorry to rush off like this, St. Ives, but we've got things to do, people to see, and plans to plot."

"You'll be around tonight, I suppose."

"Just look for the car with the flashing lights and the extra-loud siren," Fastnaught said.

They moved to the door. "St. Ives hasn't got a thing to worry about now, has he, Fastnaught?" Demeter said.

"He should be worry-proof," the Sergeant said.

"Just one item, Lieutenant," I said.

"What?" Demeter said as he opened the door.

"Try not to screw it up."

He turned from the door and let his bright black beanlike eyes run from the tips of my cordovan shoes to the top of my head where my hair lay in a neatly trimmed pile that could have been a little thicker, but was nicely touched with gray at the temples. From the expression on Demeter's face, he could have been measuring me for a casket. A cheap one. "We'll try not to screw it up, Mr. St. Ives," he said with something that almost resembled a smile. "We'll try not to very hard."

When they had gone I picked up the green telephone book and looked up a number. I dialed and when it answered, I said, "What time do you close?"

"At ten o'clock," a woman's voice said. "The stacks close at seven forty-five."

I said thank you and hung up and went to the window to see if Fastnaught had told the truth about the rain. He had so I left my raincoat hanging in the closet, took the elevator down to the lobby, and flagged a cab from the sidewalk. After I was in, the driver turned and gave me a questioning look. He wanted to know where I was headed so I said, "Library of Congress, please."

If you had enough time and enough patience, I suppose you could find out all about everything at the Library of Congress. I spent two hours in its periodical section, guided in my search by an elderly gentleman with a hearing aid who didn't mind scurrying back and forth bearing back issues of some rather esoteric and extremely dull publications. When the periodical room closed at 5:45 I went to the main reading room and spent another hour with the bound back issues of some more tedious publications which looked as if no one had leafed through them in 20 years. When I finished at 7:30 I had acquired a sizable chunk of information and some of it might even prove useful.

I caught a cab to the Hertz place, rented a four-door Ford Galaxie, and parked it in the Madison's garage. In my room I tried to call Frances Wingo at home, but there was no answer. I poured a mild Scotch and water and then telephoned down for a steak sandwich and a tall glass of milk. I chewed the sandwich and drank the milk and tasted neither. Afterwards, I stretched out on the bed and studied the ceiling and watched some thoughts go galloping through my mind, stumbling a little now and again, but galloping around and around and winding up at the same place because they had nowhere else to go.

161

17

The golf driving range was called Puckett's and it took
up several acres of gradually sloping land on Wiscon-
sin Avenue just this side of the District line. A dozen
or so golfers were trying to straighten out their hooks
and slices with big tin buckets full of balls that they
drove with varying success at markers which told
whether they were hitting 100, 150, 200, or 300 yards.
There was also a single marker that read 500 yards but
nobody seemed to pay it much attention. Giant banks
of floodlights provided almost day-bright illumina-
tion, and out in the middle of the driving range a
gasoline-powered cart covered with a steel-mesh cage
shuffled back and forth gobbling up the spent balls
like an oversized vacuum cleaner. There were more
cars than there were golfers. Some of them probably
contained people whose television sets had broken
down for the night and who would watch anything,
even 45-year-old duffers, as long as it was for free.
Some of the cars were empty and some contained lone

women who seemed resigned to a fate which had married them off to men who thought that breaking 100 at Chevy Chase ranked in historical significance with the signing of a nuclear-test-ban treaty or dinner for four at the White House.

I parked the Ford five cars down from the white wooden hut that rented the balls and clubs. I sat there, exactly on time at 10:15, with $250,000 worth of neatly wrapped, well-used tens and twenties on the back seat, and watched a man in his sixties top his ball three times in a row, and waited for someone to open the rear door and hand in a brass shield that some thought could save the lives of thousands and which had already cost the lives of four.

At ten-seventeen the lights went out. One moment the big banks of floodlights on top of the tall wooden poles bathed the driving range in a glaring yellowish white. The next moment there was nothing but blackness, made even more impenetrable by the eyes' inability to adjust. Reaction was slow. It took at least five seconds before the first horn blew. Then another. Somebody on the tee, a man, yelled, "What the hell—" and the rear door of the Ford opened. I forgot the warning and started to twist around and it may have saved my life. Something quite hard landed on the side of my head, just above the vulnerable temple, and I didn't get to see who delivered the blow in what, I later decided, was a most competent and professional manner. Nor did I have the opportunity to see who made off with a man's suitcase stuffed with a quarter of a million dollars in neatly wrapped, very negotiable currency.

When I came out of it I was lying on my back on the front seat and the first thing I saw was Demeter's face upside down above me. I twisted my head quickly and threw up on the floorboards. While I was doing that Demeter kept saying, "Are you all right, are you all right?" and I kept wanting to say, "No, I'm not all right, my head hurts like hell," but I had to throw up

163

some more instead. Finally I was through and managed to sit up. I felt the sore place on my head and the knot seemed to be not less than an inch high and two inches wide. It wasn't really that large; it only seemed so to my carefully sensitive touch. It hurt enough to be twice that large.

I leaned back in the seat and looked at Demeter, bending half crouched in the open right-hand door as if he couldn't make up his mind whether to get in.

"Are you all right?" he said again. I noticed that the lights were back on.

"No," I said. I started to turn around and look in the back seat, but I didn't because I knew it wouldn't be any use. "No shield," I said.

"No," Demeter said.

"No money either."

"No. No money."

"One of them got to the main switch."

"Probably the woman," he said.

"And the man slugged me and took the suitcase."

"That's right."

"How long were the lights off?"

"Two minutes, maybe three," he said.

"And they just drove off."

"No."

"Don't tell me you caught them?"

"If they'd left from here, we would've. We had both ends of the street sealed off."

I touched the bump on my head again. It seemed to have grown another inch. "But they didn't leave from here."

"Not exactly," he said. "From down there," and he pointed across the driving range to its far edge where the shielded cart that sucked up the golf balls rested a few feet away from the lone sign that read five hundred yards.

"How long was I out?" I said.

"Maybe ten, eleven minutes."

"How'd they do it?"

164

"They probably cased the place earlier today and found out where the main switch is. It's in a metal box outside the shack. Don't ask me why. Puckett says he locks it when he leaves at night, but he doesn't lock it while he's operating. They parked their car over there beyond those trees that are behind the five-hundred-yard marker. Walked over here and sat around watching the golf balls or even hit a few themselves until you arrived. Then she doused the lights, he slugged you, grabbed the money, and ran for the cart. That's how I figure it anyhow."

"How'd they find it in the dark?"

"The cart? They had a flashlight. I saw it out there, but I thought it was the guy in the cart. Anyway they slugged him and then drove to the edge of the range, jumped out, and now they're probably home free counting the money."

I started to shake my head but decided not to because it might hurt too much. "Clever," I said. "Where were you and the good Sergeant Fastnaught when the lights went out, if the phrase be permitted?"

"Just four cars down from you," Demeter said in a glum voice.

"Just four lousy cars away."

"That'll look good in your report."

Demeter glared at me. "Don't ride me, St. Ives."

"Have you told the museum or Mrs. Wingo?" I think he almost blushed. At least he looked embarrassed.

"No. Not yet."

I slid over the seat, under the wheel, and started the engine. "Good luck," I said.

"Where you going?"

"Well, I don't think I can lose another quarter of a million here tonight so I thought I'd go back to the hotel and order up some ice. Some of it I'll wrap in a towel and apply to my head. The rest I'll use to chill what probably will prove to be a large amount of strong drink. I'll also call Frances Wingo for you and

165

tell her how I managed to spend the museum's two hundred and fifty thousand bucks."

"Uh," Demeter said.

"Any message for her? Something reassuring like several new leads have turned up in the course of the investigation and arrests are momentarily expected? She might like that."

Demeter slammed the right door. "Go back to the hotel, St. Ives. Go back and get drunk. Roll in the gutter. But just get out of my sight."

I left.

Back in the hotel's garage I gave the attendant five dollars to clean up the mess on the front floorboards and then checked the desk for messages. There were two from Frances Wingo. I went up to my room and called her number. She answered on the second ring, as if she'd been waiting for it.

"This is St. Ives," I said.

"Yes, Mr. St. Ives," she said, "I've been in touch with Mr. Spencer and he would very much like a progress report tomorrow. Would you be free at eleven o'clock?"

"Yes, I'll be free but I don't believe I'll have much progress to report."

"Nevertheless, Mr. Spencer would like a full accounting of recent developments. You needn't mention that the police suspect that my husband engineered the theft. I've already told Mr. Spencer about that."

"What did he say?"

"I scarcely think that's any concern of yours, Mr. St. Ives. I'll expect you in my office at eleven tomorrow. Good night."

She hung up before I could tell her that I'd misplaced a quarter of a million dollars' worth of the museum's money. It was something I should have mentioned, but then I've always been one to postpone unpleasantness whenever possible. Tomorrow at eleven would be soon enough when Mr. Winfield Spencer came to town with his barber-college haircut and his billion-dollar checkbook. I could tell both of them and I could almost feel Spencer's cold green eyes boring a new hole in my head.

I called down for some ice and after it came I wrapped some of it in a towel and gently applied it to the swelling which throbbed in sharp staccato bursts of pain. I wondered if I had a concussion and tried to remember some of the symptoms. Double vision, for one. I also tried to remember whether liquor was good for a concussion and quickly convinced myself that it was. I poured a large portion into a bathroom glass, added some ice, took a reassuring swallow, and was quite set to take another when the phone rang. I picked it up and said hello.

"Mbwato, here," the familiar deep voice said. "How are you this evening, Mr. St. Ives?"

"Not too well," I said.

"Really. What's wrong?"

"Just a headache."

"Possibly brought about by nervous tension resulting from the unexpected loss of a rather large sum of money, hmmm?" And then he laughed for what seemed to be a very long time while I stood there and clutched the phone, somehow afraid that he might hang up in my ear.

When he was through laughing I said, "How did you—"

"How did I know?" he interrupted, chuckling a little, far down in his stomach. "Forgive me if I seem happy, but I think I am very close to regaining the shield for my country and when a Komporeenean is happy and successful, he likes to laugh."

"About the money," I said.

"Of course, of course. Its loss must be your immediate concern."

167

"It does bother me a little."

"Be bothered no more, Mr. St. Ives. Your money is safe and—uh—uh—"

"Sound," I said.

"That's it, sound. Strange how some clichés seem to evade one for the moment."

"Where is it safe and sound, Mr. Mbwato?" I said as my grip on the phone threatened to crack it.

"Why with me, of course," he said, and sounded a trifle surprised, even miffed, as if I'd questioned his legitimacy. "Would you like it back?" And the way he said it there was real candor, even wonder, in his tone.

"Yes, now that you mention it," I said. "I would."

"Then you shall have it. Can you come to this address?" And he gave me an address on Corcoran Place, between Q and R Streets.

"I'll catch a cab," I said.

"Oh, by the way, Mr. St. Ives," Mbwato said.

"What?"

"I have something else that might be of interest to you."

"What?"

"I have the two thieves."

18

It was a three-story row house on Corcoran Place, a narrow, one-way street running east. More properly, I suppose, it should have been called a town house because someone had gone to a lot of expense to remodel it. The brick veneer was painted an antique white and the woodwork was trimmed in flat brick. One of those stagey-looking gas lamps burned outside. I paid the cab driver, walked up seven steps, and pushed a button. Nothing happened for almost a minute and then a light went on in what I assumed to be the hall. The door opened a crack while an eye peered out at me and then it opened wide. It was the slim, dark Mr. Ulado, looking almost naked in shirt sleeves.

"Come in, Mr. St. Ives," he said. "I'm sorry I was so long in opening the door, but we're up on the third floor."

I went in and found myself in a hall that had a floor of random width pine planking that was polished to high gleam. There were a few paintings on the wall, a couple of pieces of good furniture that someone with money and taste might place in a hall, and some stairs. Mr. Ulado headed for the stairs. I followed him.

"This house," he said, "belongs to an American friend of Mr. Mbwato's who sympathizes with our cause. He and his wife are on holiday in Europe this summer and he has let us use his house as our Washington headquarters. It's a most convenient location, don't you think?"

I told him that I thought it was fine.

The carpeting on the stairs ran out on the third flight. The remodeling apparently had not risen above the second floor. There was a small landing and a door at the top of the third flight. Mr. Ulado pushed the door open and then stood to one side to let me enter. I went in and found myself in a large room that was illuminated by a single, naked bulb that hung by a cord from a fixture in the ceiling. Underneath the bulb were two straight wooden chairs and in the chairs, their backs to me, were a man and a woman. Their hands were tied to the backs of the chairs with what looked to be clothesline. Mbwato, down to shirt sleeves, stood in front of the man and the woman, staring at them as he rocked back and forth a little on his toes, his hands on his hips. He looked up when I came in.

"Mr. St. Ives, how nice," he said, and managed to make it sound as if I were the late but honored guest at the Embassy reception. "You made good time."

"I had an incentive," I said. "Two hundred and fifty thousand dollars' worth."

"Oh, yes, the money." He looked around the room vaguely. "It's over there, I believe," and he pointed to the left side of the room. The suitcase sat under a window, casually, as if someone who had just come back from a trip had placed it there because he wanted to rest a moment before unpacking.

"Thank you," I said. It was without doubt the most inadequate phrase I'd ever uttered.

Mbwato waved a huge hand, dismissing my thanks. "Think nothing of it. Come meet our two thieves. My word, but they're being most uncooperative."

I walked over to Mbwato, stood at his side, and looked down at the pair. The man was about thirty, I guessed, black-haired with long sideburns. He wore a navy turtleneck shirt with long sleeves, black slacks, and black shoes. He stared up at me with hazel eyes that had an oriental cast to them, made even more pronounced by his high cheekbones. Thin, almost colorless lips made a line underneath a sharply pointed nose. There was nothing in his face that I could see other than a kind of animal awareness that can be found in a hustling shoe clerk or a crafty checker-outer at a supermarket.

The woman, or girl, I suppose, was not much over twenty-two, if that. She wore dark slacks and a turtleneck shirt that matched her friend's. Her hair was long and straight and either brown or blond, depending on which streak you looked at. Blue eyes, an ordinary nose, and a sullen mouth did nothing to set her off from the run-of-the-mill, the not pretty, not plain girls for whom the word average was invented.

"This," Mbwato said, indicating the man, "is Jack. And this is Jill. That's all they've told us thus far, but I'm sure they'll become more cooperative as time passes."

"How'd you get them?" I said.

Ulado was bending behind the man, making sure that the knots were tight, I suppose. When he was satisfied, he checked the girl's ropes and then stood behind them, his arms folded over his chest.

"You seldom look behind you, do you, Mr. St. Ives?" Mbwato said.

"No, I suppose I don't."

"We've kept you under constant surveillance for the

171

past several days—up until today, in fact. One of my associates followed you into the Nickerson Building where the man Spellacy was murdered."

"He didn't go up the elevator with me."

"No, he didn't. He watched you as you read the building directory. Then he watched what floors the elevator stopped at. You were reading the M's and the elevator stopped on the sixth and eleventh floors. The only listing for a firm beginning with M on the sixth and eleventh floors was Mesa Verde Estates. When you came down, another of my associates picked you up and the other man rode up to the eleventh floor, popped his head into Mesa Verde Estates, and saw that Mr. Spellacy was quite dead."

"Just how many associates do you have?" I said.

Mbwato turned on his glow-in-the-dark smile. "Oh, a dozen, I think, here and in New York. Most of them are students."

"What about them?" I said, indicating the man and the girl.

"Quite by accident, I'm afraid. We were on the train that you took down from New York, in a coach, regrettably. Most uncomfortable. We followed you to the Madison and were waiting in the lobby. At least, Mr. Ulado was. He recognized the New York detective when he came in because he had already called on you at your New York hotel twice. So naturally Mr. Ulado kept his eyes on him. Our young couple here suddenly materialized in the lobby—I suppose we all took the train down from New York—and proceeded to stab Mr. Ogden, I believe his name was. So Mr. Ulado, displaying sound judgment, I should add, followed our young couple, still hoping that they would lead us to the shield. We kept them under observation all day, and followed them this evening. When they parked their car tonight at the far edge of the driving range we simply waited. When they came back, rather hurriedly, carrying the suitcase, we decided it was time to take matters in hand. And here we are."

"And they've said nothing?"

"Not yet," Mbwato said. "But our methods have been most gentle." He sighed. "I'm really disturbed that we may be forced to turn to more persuasive means."

"Such as?"

"Torture, Mr. St. Ives," he said. "The West African variety, which is, I should add for the benefit of our young friends here, most excruciating. Mr. Ulado is an expert, aren't you, Mr. Ulado?"

Mr. Ulado smiled faintly and managed to look a little embarrassed.

"Why don't you just turn them over to the police?" I said.

"The shield, Mr. St. Ives, you forget the shield. We intend to obtain it from wherever it now is."

I moved over to the man. "Your name's Jack, right?"

He said nothing, but only stared at me with his hazel eyes that seemed curiously empty, containing no fear or alarm or even regret.

"I think you'd better tell the man where the shield is, Jack."

He looked at me some more and then, quite conversationally, said, "Fuck you."

I nodded and moved over to the girl. "The man is really serious," I said. "About the torture, I mean. You'd better tell him."

Her blue eyes were empty of thought and probably of emotion, except the lustier ones like rage and hate. She smiled a little, repeated what her friend had said, and then giggled. I had heard that giggle before.

I turned to Mbwato. "They're all yours. What do you have in mind?"

Mbwato sighed. "It's really not my field, you know. I suppose we should ask Mr. Ulado. Would you care to describe your methods to our guests, Mr. Ulado?"

"Certainly," he said, walked over to the window ledge, and picked up a package about twelve inches long. He then walked back and stood before the pair.

173

"Unfortunately, we do not have all the equipment that is normally used in such instances, so we have been forced to improvise. The American drugstore is full of items that are most satisfactory substitutes. This one for instance," he said, and indicated the box. "It contains what is called a curling iron. Operating on electricity, it becomes extremely hot. And when inserted into a man's rectum or a woman's vagina, it should produce considerable pain as I will shortly demonstrate."

He took the curling iron from its box, which he dropped to the floor. The girl stared at him and then, quite suddenly, giggled. The man just looked. Ulado reached up and plugged the curling iron into the double socket that held the light. Holding the iron in his right hand, he turned to Mbwato.

"Which do you think we should begin with, sir?"

Mbwato seemed to give the question serious consideration. "I'm not sure, Mr. Ulado. What do you think, Mr. St. Ives, the gentleman or the lady?"

I shrugged. "The girl, I think."

"Very well, Mr. Ulado, the young lady."

Mr. Ulado nodded, spat on his finger, and touched it to the curling iron. The spit sizzled. "If you will just hold this for me, sir, while I prepare the woman." He handed the curling iron to Mbwato and turned to the girl.

"You're not going to stick that in me!" she screamed.

"Not if you tell us the whereabouts of the shield," Mbwato said in a genial voice. "Otherwise," and he made a slight gesture with the iron.

The girl turned her head toward the man. "I'm going to tell him."

"Shut up," the man said. "They're not going to do anything. They're just bluffing." I noticed that there was a sheen of moisture on his forehead.

"Continue, Mr. Ulado," Mbwato said.

"I will have to remove her slacks first," he said.

"Get on with it then."

"It would be better if we had a table."

"Improvise, man, improvise," Mbwato said.

"First the slacks," Ulado said, and approached the girl.

"Get away from me, you black bastard!" she yelled. "Get him away." She started to sob, deep, harsh sobs that seemed almost like coughs. "We don't have it," she screamed, "we don't have the goddamned shield."

Mbwato reached up to the light fixture, unplugged the curling iron, glanced at it distastefully, and then looked around for someplace to put it. He decided on the floor.

"Where is the shield?" Mbwato said to the girl, spacing his words carefully.

"We don't know," she said, her voice almost a moan, "we haven't got it."

"But you stole it from the museum?" Mbwato said.

"Yes, the nigger guard got it out for us. But we haven't got it. We only had it for a few minutes anyway."

Mbwato turned to the man. The thin coating of moisture that I'd seen on his forehead had turned into drops of sweat that ran down into his eyes. He tried to blink them dry.

"From the first, Jack," Mbwato said softly. "From the very first."

"Fuck you," Jack said again.

Mbwato's open palm landed against the man's cheek with a loud, wet smack. The man's stiff features seemed to crumple and I realized that he was crying. "All right," he said, "all right." He snuffled some more and turned to look at the girl. "Dumb ones," he said bitterly. "I always get dumb ones."

"From the very first," Mbwato said.

"Spellacy," the man who claimed that his name was Jack said. "He got me onto it. He knew a guy in Washington who had a real sweet one. Just walk up to a back door and somebody would hand us something worth ten thousand bucks."

"Ten thousand?" I said.

"That was our cut at first, in the beginning. Spellacy got us in touch with this guy in Washington. Wingo. A real junkie. He told us the deal. He had the guard all set up by then and the four of us met here in Washington. Those two were so junkie that you couldn't tell how they'd fly. And then Wingo started talking about two hundred and fifty thousand bucks. The ransom. So I called Spellacy and said what kind of a deal is this where my cut is ten grand out of two-fifty. So we talked it over and decided to get rid of Wingo. We just gave him an extra dose one night and let him roll down the side of the road. But then we had a problem. Wingo had been supplying the guard with H and now we had to supply him. Spellacy bought it in New York and we kept him going. The guard, I mean."

"Where was Wingo getting his stuff?" I said. "From what I hear he needed five hundred bucks a day to keep him, Sackett and Sackett's wife happy."

"I don't know where he got it," the man said. "I asked him once but he just laughed and said he had a private supply. A very private supply, he said and then laughed some more like he was crazy."

"Continue, please," Mbwato said.

"Well, shit, you know the rest. We got the shield and then we got rid of the guard. It was down to a three-way split then, me, Spellacy, and dumbie here. But what's Spellacy done? Nothing."

"So you got rid of him," I said.

"Where is the shield?" Mbwato asked.

"I don't know."

"What did you do with it?"

"It was part of the deal, the one that Wingo set up. We got it, drove about six blocks, and put it in the back seat of a car. That's the last I ever saw of it."

"The shield of Komporeen," the girl said, and giggled.

"Whose car?" Mbwato demanded.

"Christ, I don't know whose car. It was a car that was supposed to be parked at a certain place and was. I just put it in the back seat."

"I see," Mbwato said, and sighed. He turned to me. "We seem to have solved a few murders and a theft, Mr. St. Ives. But we are no closer to the shield."

"I'm not sure," I said. "As long as he's in a talkative mood, I'd like to clear up something. What about Lieutenant Ogden, Jack? How'd he get on to you?"

"Spellacy," he said dully. "Ogden found out about you being interested in Spellacy and he figured that Spellacy was in on the deal. And if he knew Spellacy was in, he knew I was in. Spellacy and me worked together a lot. And Ogden knew me, too. Christ, he should have. I paid him off enough times because of dumb broads like her."

"Did he get in touch with you?"

"He tried to; he got the word around that he was looking for me. Ah, to hell with him. He's dead." He looked up and smiled at me. "We sure had you on the run though, buster, didn't we?"

"That's right," I said, "you sure did."

"All on account of some goddamned shield."

"The shield of Komporeen," the girl said, and gave us the pleasure of listening to another one of her giggles.

19

Mbwato and I left Mr. Ulado to look after his two charges while we went downstairs to sample the town-house owner's Scotch. I carried the suitcase in my right hand. It didn't seem to weigh as much as it once had and I wondered whether I should count the money, but decided not to because there wasn't much I could do about it if some were missing—certainly not replace it.

Mbwato mixed two drinks and we sat in the comfortable living room that contained some more pictures, some better than average furniture, and a large number of books. I sat on the couch, Mbwato in the largest chair he could find, which still seemed too small for his bulk.

"So, Mr. St. Ives, what shall I do with our two young friends upstairs?"

"Turn them over to the cops."

"Do you think they're sane?"

"The man is, I think. I don't know about the girl. She seems a little kinky, but maybe it's like he said, she's just dumb."

"Rather coarse, too," Mr. Mbwato murmured.

"Well, not quite as coarse as a hot curling iron. Tell me something, is Ulado really your torture expert?"

Mbwato chuckled. "Good heavens no, man. Couldn't you see that he was absolutely petrified? He got the idea from one of your more lurid magazines, I think. Still, it proved quite effective, didn't it?"

"Suppose they hadn't talked. Suppose they were stubborn. Would you have used it?"

Mbwato gave me a long, speculative look. "Let me reply in this fashion: would you have tried to stop me?"

I nodded. "I guess so."

"And you would have succeeded." He sighed deeply. "The threat was all that was really needed. Their lives have conditioned them to accept quite readily the notion that two black African savages would think nothing of torturing them for hours on end. They have been indoctrinated by their culture to accept this."

"Too many Tarzan films, huh?" I said.

"I'm not so sure about that. It's just that if the roles were reversed, neither of them would have had any compunction about using the iron on me or Mr. Ulado. So they quite readily accepted the fact that we would torture them." He sighed again. "But what to do with them?"

"The cops," I said.

"Really, Mr. St. Ives."

"Why not?"

"Could it be done—say—anonymously?"

"Well, you can't just mail them downtown in a plain wrapper."

"Could you possibly..."

"Possibly," I said.

"I would be most grateful."

"Not as grateful as I am for getting the money back. I haven't thanked you adequately."

Mbwato put his drink down on a table and leaned forward, resting his arms on his knees. He studied the carpet. "The money is more important to you than the shield, isn't it?"

"I suppose so. If I return the money to the museum, then they're right back where they started. I can bow out and that's the end of it."

"And that's what you intend to do tomorrow?" he said.

"No," I said, "I don't intend to do that at all."

He looked up at me. "What then?"

"I intend to get the shield back."

His eyes widened. Big as saucers, I thought, like the troll's who lived under the bridge and had a good thing going until Big Billy Goat Gruff came along.

"You know where it is?"

I took a long time before answering. "Possibly," I said.

"Probably?" he said.

"Yes."

"My earlier offer still stands, Mr. St. Ives."

"Forget it," I said.

"You have a better one?"

"No."

Mbwato rose and began to pace the floor in long strides. "You're being most infuriating with your hints and allusions, Mr. St. Ives. You know that, I suppose."

"I hadn't thought about it," I said. "I'm sorry."

He stopped his pacing and stood before me, bending forward slightly, a huge, very black man whose broad, curiously gentle face was a battleground for hope and despair. Despair seemed to be winning. "I do not mind the personal disgrace that will accompany my failure," he said. "I hope you understand that; I hope you believe it."

"I believe it," I said.

"You realize the importance of the shield—not to me personally, but to my country."

"You've told me about it. Twice, in fact. Maybe three times."

"Then I need not repeat it."

"No."

"Now you say you intend to get the shield back."

"That's right."

"How?"

"Don't you mean where?" I said.

"All right. Where?"

"I don't know. I'm still just guessing. All I really know is that I'll need some help."

"Is that a request?" Mbwato said softly.

I nodded. I was tired. I wanted to go to bed. My head had started to throb again, worse than before. "You can call it that," I said.

"When will you need it?"

"Tomorrow at the latest."

"What do you intend to do with the shield, Mr. St. Ives, return it to the museum?"

"I don't have it yet. I might not ever have it. As I said, I'm only guessing. The only thing that I really know is I've been suckered and I'm not quite sure by whom. Maybe by you. Maybe by the museum or my lawyer or even Lieutenant Demeter and his faithful Sergeant Fastnaught. Maybe it's all been some kind of gigantic conspiracy that everybody's been in on except me. Or maybe it's just that I have a slight concussion and it's done something to my brain. Turned me a little paranoic." My head was no longer throbbing; it was pounding and the pain hit at the back of my head where it hadn't been before.

"No more questions, Mr. Mbwato," I said. "No more questions because I haven't got the answers. Right now the only thing I want to do is go home and go to bed. But I can't even do that because I have to call the cops and hand over your two friends upstairs." I slumped back on the couch, but it only made my head hurt more. "Can you clear out of here?"

"Yes, of course," Mbwato said.

"Where can I reach you tomorrow?" I wasn't looking at him; I had my eyes closed, but that didn't ease the pain either.

"Here," he said, "at this number." He produced one of his ivory-colored cards and scribbled a telephone number on it. He handed it to me and I shoved it into my coat pocket.

"What time do you think you may—"

"I don't know. I told you I don't know anything. I'm just guessing. Maybe I won't call at all. Maybe it'll all blow up in my face. Bang, like that. Or Boom. Or even bang-boom."

"Are you feeling all right, Mr. St. Ives?" Mbwato said, and there seemed to be genuine solicitation in his voice, or it could have been that he was just worried about the shield and that I might die on him.

"No," I said. "I'm not feeling all right. Where's the phone?"

"At your elbow."

"So it is," I said, and because it seemed to sound nice, I said it again. "So it is. Another drink might help, Mr. Mbwato. Another touch of your landlord's excellent Scotch. And as soon as that is done, I suggest that you gather up Mr. Ulado and flee into the night. Just make sure that our two young friends upstairs are securely bound."

"Yes," he said, handing me another drink. "I'll see to it. Is there anything I can do for you, Mr. St. Ives? You don't seem at all well. I might even say that you look pale, but then I'm no great judge."

"I'm tiptop," I said. "Both the tip and the top of my head are about to sail off."

"I'll get Mr. Ulado," he said, and headed for the stairs.

I picked up the phone and dialed Lieutenant Demeter's number. He answered with his usual "Robbery Squad, Lieutenant Demeter," but most of the bark and bite were missing.

"How goes the report, Lieutenant?"

"What do you want, St. Ives?"

"A word or two with you. Only a word or two."

"You drunk?"

"Possibly, possibly. My head is coming off and seems to be sailing around the room."

"You're drunk," he said.

"The two thieves, Lieutenant. I have them bound and gagged. Well, not gagged really, but bound. Yes, bound with strong cord. And the money too. A quarter of a million dollars. I have recovered it. Do you find that interesting?"

There was a silence for a moment and then Demeter said, "Is this a joke, St. Ives?"

"If it were, it wouldn't be a very good one, would it? No joke. Thieves and money. They're both here. I thought I'd call before you got too far into your report."

"Where are you?"

I took another swallow of my drink, a large one. The pain in my head now seemed focused behind my eyes, threatening to push them out of their sockets. I closed them. "In a charming town house on Corcoran Place."

"The address, goddammit."

"Oh, yes." I gave him the address.

"If this is some kind of a joke—"

"No joke," I said. "No joke at all." I hung up.

Mbwato and Ulado came down the stairs and entered the living room. Both now wore coats and ties. Ulado crossed over to me and put some items on the coffee table. "We relieved them of these," he said. "I thought that they might be evidence—or something like that." On the coffee table were two switchblade knives, a .38-caliber revolver, and blackjack with a spring handle.

"We're leaving now, Mr. St. Ives," Mbwato said. "Is

there anything I can do for you?"

I waved my empty glass at him. "Another drink to cut the phlegm."

Ulado hurried forward and took my glass, looking at Mbwato, who nodded. "You need to sleep, Mr. St. Ives," he said.

"I know," I said. "For a couple of years."

"I'll be anticipating your call tomorrow," he said as Ulado handed me the fresh drink.

"Man your phone," I said. "I shall be calling."

Mr. Mbwato stood by the door to the hall and stared at me. "I hope, Mr. St. Ives, that you know what you're doing."

"I hope so, too, Mr. Mbwato," I said. "I hope so very much."

20

The pain had eased a little by the time that Demeter and Fastnaught arrived. Perhaps the Scotch had helped after all, or it may have been because I had stopped thinking about what I had to do the next day. The thoughts had been more than unpleasant; they had been nasty ones born of apprehension and dread and they had burrowed into my mind like a small, wet furry animal with stainless-steel teeth and claws that scratched and chomped around in my head. The giddiness had gone, too, and when I answered the police-like banging on the door I was as sober and composed as one could hope to be on four very large drinks.

"There's a bell," I said when I opened the door, "or don't you believe in them?"

"He's drunk," Demeter said. "You can smell it."

"Come in, gentlemen. All by yourselves, I see."

"If this is a joke, St. Ives, we want to enjoy it in private," Demeter said, and pushed himself past me into the hall. Fastnaught followed, chewing on a stick of gum. His eyes looked more bloodshot than usual.

"You look like hell," Fastnaught said.

"I've got a headache, but it's better now."

"All right," Demeter said. "What's the story?"

"Jack and Jill are upstairs on the third floor," I said. "Jack and Jill are the thieves. They're also the murderers, as nasty a young couple as our stricken society has yet produced."

Demeter stared at me suspiciously. "Just sitting there waiting for us, huh?"

"They're all tied up," I said. "Securely."

"Okay, let's check it out, Fastnaught," Demeter said. He produced a revolver from a shoulder holster and waved it vaguely toward the stairs. Fastnaught also drew his revolver and started up the stairs, chewing his gum. "You coming, St. Ives?" Demeter said.

"Too far," I said. "Far too far. And I've got a headache."

I watched them slowly mount the stairs until they were out of sight on the second-floor landing. Then I went back into the living room and poured myself another drink, mentally assigning it curative powers that would have done credit to a dozen or so of the more progressive wonder drugs. I sat on the couch and waited. A few moments later there was a sharp sound as if someone had kicked in a door. Or maybe they had just banged it open against the wall. I took a sip of my drink and waited some more. In a few minutes I could hear them descending the stairs. Fastnaught came in first, his gun still drawn. He was followed by the girl with her hands handcuffed behind her. Then came the man, also handcuffed, and Demeter, still with his revolver in his hand.

"Ah, you caught them, Lieutenant," I said. "Good work."

"Shut up," Demeter said.

Fastnaught turned and waved his gun at two chairs. "Sit down over there," he said to the girl and the man.

They moved over to the two chairs and sat down.

"The suitcase with the money is by that chair," I said.

"I saw it," Demeter said, reholstering his gun. "You count it?"

"No. Should I've?"

"Didn't you even look?"

"No."

"Take a look, Fastnaught."

Fastnaught bent over the suitcase, turned it on its side, and opened it. The tens and twenties were still there, wrapped in neat brown paper bands.

"Jesus," Fastnaught said, and I felt that there was pure reverence in his tone.

"All right, close it up," Demeter said. He turned to me. "Now tell us all about it, St. Ives."

"I got a call at my hotel, an anonymous tip. He said that the thieves and the money were at this address, all safe and sound. So I caught a cab over, found it to be just like the man on the phone said, and then called you."

"You lying son of a bitch," said the man who claimed that his name was Jack. "The big niggers got us. They talked funny, like Englishmen. They were going to shove a curling iron up my ass if I didn't tell 'em and he was gonna help."

"Tell what?" Demeter said.

The man called Jack looked away. "Nothing. I don't have to tell you nothing. But he's a lying son of a bitch."

"Strange," I said. "They were both extremely talkative a few minutes ago. They were telling me how they had managed to steal the shield and do away with four persons—Sackett, Wingo, Spellacy, and your former classmate, Lieutenant Ogden."

Demeter slipped his revolver back into its holster, looked around the room, picked out a chair, and eased himself into it slowly. He reached into the inside pocket of his jacket, found a cigar encased in a metal tube, and went through the ritual of lighting it. When it was well lighted he looked at me with black, beany eyes. "Nothing like a good cigar," he said.

"That suitcase would buy a lot of them," I said.

"What do you think, Fastnaught?" Demeter said to the sergeant, who had also tucked away his gun and was now leaning against the mantel of the fireplace, which looked as if it really worked.

"About what?" Fastnaught said.

"Do you think the suitcase would buy a lot of cigars?"

"Plenty," Fastnaught said.

"Cigars for me, little girls for you, and punchboards for St. Ives here."

"What about our two friends here, Jack and Jill?" I said.

"I don't think their names are Jack and Jill really. What'd Ogden tell you just before he died? He said something about 'Freddie and his whore,' didn't he?" Demeter turned to look at the man in handcuffs. "Are you Freddie and his whore, son?" he asked mildly.

Freddie, or Jack, told Demeter to go fuck himself. Fastnaught sighed, left his spot at the mantel, crossed over to the man and struck him twice across the face with an open palm. Fastnaught seemed neither to like nor dislike striking the man. He said nothing after he had done it and a moment later he was back leaning against the mantel, rubbing a corner of it into the spot between his shoulder blades where the itch seemed to persist. The man's face had crumpled again and I saw that he was crying. He didn't like being hit.

"I asked you a question, son," Demeter said. "Is your name Freddie?"

The man sat with his head bowed. He was almost through crying. The girl looked at him blankly and then giggled.

"Fred," he said.

"Fred what?"

"Fred Simpson."

"All right, Fred Simpson, what about the girl? She your wife?"

"No."

"He's my pimp," the girl said. "He's my pretty little pimp. Freddie the pimp." She giggled again.

"What's your name, lady?" Demeter said.

"Wanda."

"Wanda what?"

"Wanda Lou Wesoloski."

"A Polack," Freddie said. "A dumb Polack."

"Tell us about it, Freddie," Demeter said.

"I want a lawyer. I don't have to say nothing."

"That's right, Freddie, you don't," Demeter said, and shifted his gaze to me. "You say that Freddie was talkative a little earlier?"

"Extremely," I said.

"You sort of just breezed over it before, St. Ives. Why don't you let us have it again with a little more detail?"

"All right," I said, and I told them what Freddie had said as Mbwato stood there, looking for some place to put the curling iron. I didn't mention either Mbwato or Mr. Ulado. For some reason I always thought of the slim, dark young man as *Mister* Ulado.

When I was through Demeter grunted, looked for some place to dump his ash, and found a tray on a table next to him. "And Freddie here told you all that, huh? You must have been a hell of a good reporter at one time, St. Ives."

"Just fair," I said. "People confide in me."

"He's a lying bastard," Freddie said in a dull tone. "There were two niggers. They had a curling iron. He was gonna help them shove it up—ask her. Ask Wanda."

"What about it, Wanda?"

The girl looked at him blankly. "What?"

"Was there a curling iron and two spades?"

"Uh-huh," she said. "Sure. And the shield of Komporeen." She giggled again.

189

Demeter sighed. "Like I said, that suitcase would buy a lot of cigars. How much is a third of two hundred and fifty thousand, Fastnaught?"

"I've already figured it out," Fastnaught said. "It's $83,333.33."

"Sounds like a lot of money," Demeter said. "Sound like enough to you, St. Ives?"

"What happens to your two friends over there?"

"I guess they could try to escape. But like I said, is $83,333.33 enough?"

"Not for me," I said.

"I didn't think it would be," he said. "Not for a New York go-between. When you come right down to it, it's not even enough for a Washington cop." He turned to Freddie. "What kind of car did you put the shield in, Freddie?"

"I don't know what kind of car it—" He stopped quickly. "I don't have to talk to you," he said. "I gotta right to get a lawyer."

Demeter rose. "You'll need one," he said. "A good one. On your feet; we're going to take a little ride. Bring the suitcase, Fastnaught."

"Don't you think that should go back to the museum?" I said.

"What's the matter, St. Ives, you worried that maybe a hundred and twenty-five thousand each might be enough for a couple of cops?"

"I don't worry about anything," I said.

"I bet. Let me make something clear. The money is the only evidence we got. Without the money all we got is your song and dance about what these two told you. And that's hearsay. Now I'm going to call the Wingo woman when we get down to headquarters and tell her that we've got the money and two suspects. Are you happy now?"

"I'm happy," I said.

"Let's go," Demeter said.

Fastnaught moved over to the handcuffed couple and jerked his head at the door. I was on my feet and when Freddie drew abreast of me, he stopped. "Whyn't you tell 'em about the two niggers, man? Why d'you have to be such a lying son of a bitch?"

"I don't know what you're talking about, Freddie."

His face started to crumple and I thought he would cry again. But he didn't. "You lie, man!" he shouted. "You lie."

"Oh, shut up, Freddie," the girl said.

"Let's go," Fastnaught said to the pair, and herded them out through the door into the hall.

Demeter paused at the door. "You want a ride, St. Ives?"

"No thanks," I said.

"You got a date downtown at ten tomorrow, you know."

"I know."

He nodded. "You can see homicide first and then drop by my office. I'll need a statement, too."

"All right."

"Tell me something," he said.

"What?"

"Were you and the two spades really going to shove a hot curling iron up the kid's kiester?"

"I don't know anything about a curling iron, Lieutenant. Or two spades."

He nodded and puffed on his cigar twice. "Tell me something else. Just how big would it have to be for a three-way split? I mean for a big-time New York go-between."

"I don't know," I said. "How big would it have to be for a robbery-squad lieutenant?"

"I don't know either," he said. "I don't really know. I hope to God I never find out."

21

The humidity must have been nudging the hundred mark the next morning when I came out of the Metropolitan Police Headquarters at 300 Indiana Avenue. Gray, fat clouds moved slowly to the east, taking their time like plump brokers on the way back to the office after a big lunch and a thoughtful speech. It was 11:15 and I was late and there was a tickle in my throat because I had been answering questions for a solid hour and some of my answers had even bordered on the truth.

I hailed a taxi and it deposited me at the entrance of the Coulter Museum at 11:27. At 11:30 Frances Wingo's young Negro secretary was holding open the door to her employer's office. There was no smile this time. I decided that she handed out that smile only to the prompt.

At four o'clock that morning, as I lay in a rough nest of twisted sheets, it had all seemed unambiguous, clear-cut, even simple. But as I went through the door into Frances Wingo's office everything crumbled and what had seemed simple in that awful hour between four and five in the morning, now seemed impossibly far-fetched and complicated.

Frances Wingo and Winfield Spencer were seated at the far end of her office occupying two of the chairs in the cluster of comfortable furniture that was grouped around the fireplace. I noticed that the Klee was gone. In its place was a chilly blaze of electric blue squares by someone I failed to recognize. Frances Wingo wore an off-white dress that was trimmed in black. Spencer wore what seemed to be the same gray suit with vest that I'd seen him in before. His shirt collar was unfrayed this time, but his hair still seemed to have been trimmed with the garden shears. He also had on a different tie, a blue polka dot butterfly bow that clipped neatly on to his collar. It must have cost all of seventy-five cents. They both wore those politely pained, frosty expressions that are adopted by busy persons who have been kept waiting for half an hour by someone who isn't busy.

"Sorry I'm late," I said. "I had to give the police two statements and it took longer than I thought it would."

"While we were waiting," Frances Wingo said, "I informed Mr. Spencer about the call that I received from Lieutenant Demeter at one o'clock this morning. He told me about apprehending the two suspected thieves and recovering the money. It would seem that you might have let me know that the money was missing when we spoke on the phone last night, Mr. St. Ives."

"I would have," I said, "but you hung up in my ear."

Spencer once again fixed his green gaze on my forehead. "If I understand correctly, the money is safe, the thieves are caught, but the shield is still missing. That is a brief but I hope succinct summary of the current situation, is it not, Mr. St. Ives?"

"It is," I said.

"Then it would seem that you did what you said you would not do."

"What?"

"Help catch the thieves."

"Yes, it does seem that way, doesn't it?"

Spencer nodded and shifted his gaze to the coffee table that lay between the two of them in their chairs and me on the couch. "We are, of course, deeply disappointed."

"I'm sure you must be."

"The shield—not the money, not the thieves—but the shield was the most important thing."

"Yes," I said. "It would appear so."

My head started to throb again, not as bad as the night before, only a dull, deep throb—something like a distant artillery barrage.

"Our problems are further compounded," Frances Wingo said, "by the impossibility of keeping the theft from the press any longer. After I informed the Jandolaean Embassy this morning, they insisted that the news be released."

"That's understandable," I said. "Who's going to announce it?"

"I regret that we must," she said.

"When?"

"This afternoon. I've scheduled a press conference. A spokesman for the Metropolitan Police will be on hand, as will a representative of the Jandolaean Embassy."

"Isn't that a little unusual?" I said.

"Yes, but I think you'll agree that the circumstances are unusual."

I looked around for an ashtray, but found none. Frances Wingo, once more reading my mind, crossed to her desk and came back with one, which she placed on the table before me. I lit a cigarette and ignored the mild look of disapproval that appeared on Spencer's face. It only made him look a trifle more forbidding than normal.

"As thefts go it was unusual," I said. "Very unusual. Four people were killed—five if you count the guard's wife who hanged herself. That made it unusual enough to assure it a biennial spread in *True Detective* for years to come. But what made it really unusual was that there was never any thought of returning the shield. At least not to the museum."

Spencer chuckled. I had never even seen him smile so the chuckle caught me off guard. It sounded dry and dusty, as if he used it once or twice a year at most, perhaps at Christmas Eve. "Sorry," he said, "but I'm just recalling that rather lengthy lecture that you gave us when we first approached you about serving as our intermediary. At that time you went to great pains to disavow your responsibility for either the apprehension of the thieves or the solution of the theft. But it seems that last night you actually turned the two thieves, a man and a woman, I understand, over to the police and now you are displaying a certain amount of deductive reasoning in the most Holmesian manner to explain the motive behind the theft. I'm sorry, Mr. St. Ives, but I find it amusing. Why not play your new role to the hilt and tell us that you have deduced where the shield is?"

I ignored him. It's not easy to ignore a billion dollars, but I did my best. "The theft was planned by Mrs. Wingo's late husband," I said.

"That's not true," she said, but there wasn't much conviction in her voice.

"I think it's true," I said. "The police think it's true and the two thieves know it's true. They told me so last night. Your husband never intended to return the shield to the museum. He did intend to grab the ransom money though. His share would have kept him in heroin for a while and after that, there was always the chance for blackmail."

"Whom would he blackmail, Mr. St. Ives?" Spencer said.

"The person that he stole the shield for."

"And I assume that this unnamed person now has the shield?"

"Yes."

"Remarkable."

"Not really."

"So all we need is the name of the person and we can turn him over to the police."

"That's right," I said.

"And you no doubt know who this person is?"

"I think so," I said.

"You think so; you're not sure?"

"Fairly sure."

"Would you tell us?"

"No," I said. "I'll tell you, Mr. Spencer, and then, as chairman of the museum's executive board, you can determine what steps to take. But Mrs. Wingo was married to the man who planned and engineered the theft. As such she comes under suspicion as either an accomplice or an accessory."

"That is ridiculous," she said.

"Not ridiculous," I said. "Not even farfetched. Your husband had an expensive habit. He had exhausted all funds—both yours and his—and this was the only way that he could get more. A lot more. As director of the museum, you were in a position to introduce him, casually I assume, to Sackett, the guard. From there on he handled it all except that you were also in a position to tell him about that one door that wasn't electrically sealed from the inside. The police say it was an inside job. Perhaps they just haven't figured out how deeply inside it was."

She stared at me and there was nothing but contempt and loathing in her gaze. I smiled at her, but it was a feeble smile. "It does hang together, you'll have to admit."

"You mentioned that you *thought* that you know who now has the shield," Spencer said.

"I also said that I'd tell you, but not Mrs. Wingo. If she is an accomplice, and if I'm right about who has the shield, she could easily tip him off."

"You don't believe that *she* has it, do you?" Spencer said. "Tucked away in the attic perhaps, where she can admire it, even gloat over it, during long winter evenings." He chuckled again for the second time that year.

"No," I said. "I don't believe that."

"Well, Mr. St. Ives, let's get it over with. My dear, if you'll excuse yourself."

She rose and without looking at me or saying anything walked quickly to the door, opened it, and left. Spencer watched her leave. After the door closed he looked at me and this time his green eyes met mine for the first time and held.

"All right, St. Ives. Who?"

I took a deep breath, but it came out as a croak anyway. "You," I said. "You've got the shield."

197

22

At 4:36 that morning, alone in my hotel room, it had been a much better scene. Spencer had blanched, confounded by the inescapable logic of my accusation. A few drops of perspiration had formed on his upper lip. A tiny vein had started to throb in his temple. Afraid that his hands would develop a telltale tremor, he had thrust them deep into his pockets. Guilt had seeped from every pore and its odor lay heavy in the room. That was at 4:36 A.M. At 11:47 A.M. he did nothing of the kind. For a moment he looked a trifle disappointed, but politely managed to cover that up. His eyes moved away from mine, as if embarrassed. Not for him, but for me.

"I see," he murmured, and then looked around the room as though he hoped to find something else to talk about, something that would help us both pretend that I wasn't an utter fool.

It occurred to me then that I would have never made a good cop. There was something lacking. My concept of crime and punishment was skewed. Vengeance was not mine. I was cheerleader for the crooks and a cynic when it came to law and order. And finally, somewhere along the unimproved secondary road that was my life, I had discarded proper veneration for The Job at Hand, a veneration shared in common by all good crooks, cops, and, for that matter, county agents. As a go-between I was an economic grasshopper, a social cipher who in one breath had just accused a billion dollars of being a thief and was about to apologize in the next.

"It all works out," I said lamely.

"Really," Spencer said, not at all interested, gazing out the window at the Capitol and frowning slightly as if he thought it could use a new coat of paint.

"First," the Relentless Inquisitor continued, "you were one of the few persons who knew that George Wingo was an addict. You also knew that he was desperate for money to feed his habit."

"Mmm," Spencer said, getting really interested now.

"Second," I said, "you had enough money to feed it. I don't know who suggested that he get the guard hooked. I don't think it matters. At least not to me. But in Wingo you had your engineer and in Sackett your inside man. Through a man named Spellacy in New York Wingo found the thieves. And your go-between.

"Third, motive," I said.

This time Spencer smiled slightly. "Ah, yes, Mr. St. Ives. Motive. I did have one, didn't I?"

"Yes."

"Let me guess," he said. "I suddenly became totally captivated by the shield, by this crude, tawdry piece of brass. I had to possess it at all costs. It was an obsession. That seems to be in keeping with the rest of your rather fanciful ramblings."

"No," I said. "It was Eldorado."

"Ah," he said. "Eldorado."

"Eldorado Oil and Gas. It's one of your companies."

"Yes."

"Before the revolution in Jandola broke out it was negotiating for mineral rights. Oil. A lot of it and most of it is under what some call Komporeen. The Library of Congress was most helpful."

"I see."

"Now the real villain enters. Your villain anyway. It's a Dutch-British combine. It was after the oil rights, too, and it offered the Jandolaean government a far better deal. You matched it. The combine topped your offer and the Jandolaeans sat back content to let you fight it out. In the midst of the negotiations, the revolution broke out and because the oil reserves or whatever you call them are in Komporeen, the negotiations for the rights came to a standstill. I am correct so far?"

"In a crude way," Spencer said.

"For a while it looked as if the Jandolaeans would finish the fight in a week. But it dragged on. The Komporeeneans fought better than was expected. Some help started coming in dribbles from France and Germany. If the Komporeeneans could hold on another two months or so, they might even win independence. Or at least, with recognition from France or Germany, keep the fighting going for years, and if they did, then you would have to negotiate with their government. If they lost, you'd be back where you started, bidding against the Dutch-British combine. You needed an edge. And the shield was it. You knew its importance to both Komporeen and Jandola. You would arrange for its theft, and then at the appropriate time, use it as a bribe to secure the oil reserves from whoever won."

"And how would I explain that it came into my possession?" Spencer asked.

"Simple," I asked. "You bought it from the thieves, using your own money."

"I see," Spencer said again, and stared out the window some more.

"I don't think you had anything to do with the four deaths," I said.

"Thank you."

"They just got greedy and after the deal was set up, they followed it because they didn't know what else to do. None of them was too imaginative. They stole the shield, dumped it into the back seat of a car, and it was whisked away to you. None of them knew that you were involved. No one but Wingo knew that."

"But you think that you do?"

"I know you are."

"And your next move?"

"I could do several things," I said. "First of all, I could tell the cops. They might laugh at me at the beginning, but they'd check it out. It might take a while, but they'd get around to it and even if they never proved it, it would be a considerable nuisance to you. But that's just one thing that I might do. The other would be to let the Jandolaean Embassy in on my speculations. That would really tear it for you. You could never use the shield as a bribe then. They'd know you'd stolen it—or had had it stolen."

Spencer rose from his chair and crossed to the window. He stood there in his 1939 suit and his bowl haircut, a billion dollars on the hoof, and looked out at the Capitol. "How much do you want, St. Ives?" he said.

"Not how much, but what."

"All right then. What?"

"The shield. I want it today."

There was perhaps fifteen seconds of silence. I assumed that he was rapidly weighing it all, totting up the costs, figuring the losses, poking at the loopholes. He turned from the window. "What do you intend to do with it?" he said.

"That's no longer your concern."

"I can, of course, beat any price."

"I'm sure."

"So it's not price?"

201

"No."

"Then I don't understand it."

"No," I said. "I didn't think you would."

"What assurance do I have that you will continue your silence?"

"None."

"Yes," he said. "I did expect that." He thought some more, for all of five seconds. "Eight o'clock tonight."

"All right," I said. "Where?"

"My home in Virginia. It's not far from Warrenton." He spent thirty seconds giving me directions. I wrote them down.

"You will come alone, of course?" he said.

"No."

Spencer didn't like that. He frowned his frown, pursed his lips, and jutted his chin. "I must be assured some measure of privacy, Mr. St. Ives."

"Four, maybe five persons have died because of the $250,000 ransom for that shield, Mr. Spencer. According to the financial and oil and gas journals that I went through at the Library of Congress, the oil underneath Komporeen is worth maybe $200 billion or more. I guarantee that the person that I'll bring with me won't violate what you call your privacy. He will, however, make me feel a little more secure."

"He's not of the police, is he?"

"No, he's not a cop. He's just insurance as far as I'm concerned."

"And you really think you need it—this insurance?"

"Yes," I said. "I really think I do."

I was back in my hotel room by twelve-fifteen dialing the phone. A voice, a deep familiar one, answered on the first ring with a bass hello.

"Mbwato?"

"Mr. St. Ives. How good of you to call."

"You'll get your shield at eight o'clock tonight."

There was a long silence. "You are positive?"

"I'm not even positive that the earth isn't flat."

His deep laugh rolled over the phone. "According to our legends, it is a cube."

"Stick with them," I said.

"Yes," he said, and there was another pause. "There is a saying in your country about a gift horse."

"It's no gift," I said. "I've got a price."

"You restore my faith in human nature."

"I thought I would."

"And your price?"

"Six hundred and eighty-five dollars. Those are my out-of-pocket expenses."

"You are joking, of course."

"No, I'm not joking."

"No," he said slowly, "I don't think you are."

"There's one more thing."

"Yes."

"How soon can you get yourself and the shield out of the country?"

"Tonight," he said. "We have several contingency plans."

"Have you got one for Virginia?" I said.

"I beg your pardon?"

"Virginia. That's where we pick up the shield. Near Warrenton."

"And you think we may be in a hurry?"

"Yes."

"A great hurry?"

"Yes."

"To use your country's parlance, might it even be called a getaway?"

God, he likes to talk, I thought. "It could be called that."

"Then give me the exact location and I'll get Mr. Ulado on to it. He's our getaway expert. Quite good at it really."

I read him the directions that Spencer had given me. "I have a rented car in the garage here," I said. "We'll use that."

"Shall I meet you there?"

"Yes. At seven."

"Anything else?" Mbwato asked.

"Nothing."

"There are a couple of details I should attend to."

"All right," I said.

There was another pause and I was wishing he would say good-by, but he didn't. "I'm sorry, Mr. St. Ives, but my curiosity is overwhelming. Just why are you doing this when you were so adamant previously?"

"I changed my mind."

"But why?"

"Cotton candy," I said.

"I beg your pardon."

"I'm a sucker for cotton candy. Spun sugar. Just like I'm a sucker for stories about hungry kids and lost puppies and sick kittens. But after a while you get tired of listening to the stories, just like you get tired of eating cotton candy. I'm tired of your stories so I'm going to do something about it."

Then I hung up before he could tell me any more of them.

23

We only got lost once on the way out of Washington. It's an easy town to get lost in and we took a wrong turn somewhere around the Lincoln Memorial and wound up heading for Baltimore. Mbwato was navigating with the aid of an Esso map and finally he said, "I think we're headed the wrong way, old man."

Having just seen the BALTIMORE—STRAIGHT AHEAD sign I agreed with him, made what I was sure was an illegal U-turn, and headed back toward the Lincoln Memorial. This time I crossed the Memorial Bridge into Virginia, found the double-laned Washington Memorial Parkway, sped past the entrance to the CIA, and finally picked up 495, the circumferential highway that belts Washington. It was still muggy, the air conditioning in the rented Ford didn't work, and I was in a foul mood. Getting lost does that to me.

Mbwato, on the other hand, held his large black leather attaché case on his lap, hummed to himself, and admired the countryside. "According to the map," he said, "we take 495 until we come to Interstate 66, which leads to State 29 and 211. Five miles this side of Warrenton we turn right."

"In the glove compartment," I said, "there's a pint of whisky."

He opened the glove compartment, looked, and closed it. "So there is," he said.

"Would you mind kind of taking the cap off and passing it to me? I mean if it's no bother?"

"Oh, none at all," he said, got the whisky out, took off the cap, and handed me the bottle. I took a long drink and handed it back to him. "Not that I approve of drinking while driving, you understand," he said.

"I understand," I said. "Neither do I."

"But under certain circumstances, especially when there may be some unpleasantness in the offing, it should be permissible."

"Even for navigators," I said.

"That's what I thought," he said, and tilted the bottle up.

It gurgled at least three times before he put it back into the glove compartment.

He stared out at the scenery again. There wasn't much to see. Some fields, some trees, and occasionally the tacky back yard of some plastic houses that people bought because it was all they could afford and the forty-five-minute drive to Washington was a small price to pay for having lily-white neighbors.

"They didn't get quite this far, as I remember," Mbwato said.

"Who, the Negroes?"

"What Negroes?"

"Never mind," I said. "Who didn't get this far?"

"The Confederacy."

"About as close as they got was Dranesville," I said. "They turned north there toward Pennsylvania. Dranesville's about fifteen miles or so from Washington."

"I wish I had more time," he said. "I would so liked to have spent several days studying the battlefields. I'm quite a Civil War buff, you know."

"I've been to Gettysburg," I said. "I found it all very confusing."

"Were you ever a soldier, Mr. St. Ives?" he said.

"A long time ago," I said. "The war was called a police action then and I wasn't a very good soldier even in that."

"When I studied your Civil War at Sandhurst, I must confess that I developed a rather sneaking sympathy for the Confederacy. Pity that they didn't have a more suitable cause."

"It was the only cause around."

"Still, I find many parallels between the Confederacy and my own country. Both the South and Komporeen, if my history serves me right, could be described as underdeveloped, largely agricultural, but possessed of a fierce regional pride. And jealous of tradition, too, I suppose."

"And gracious living," I said. "A good, unreconstructed Southerner can go on for hours about gracious living. You know, crinoline and fatback. Myths die hard in the South and from what you've told me, they die even harder in Komporeen."

"Yes, I suppose you could call the aura that surrounds the shield a myth. But when you have very little else, myths become important, even vital."

"When were you at Sandhurst?" I said.

"From 'fifty-five to 'fifty-nine. I think I may have neglected to mention it, but I'm a lieutenant colonel in our army."

"You neglected to mention it," I said. "How many generals do you have?"

"None. There is only Colonel Aloko, who is now head of state, and three other lieutenant colonels."

"What are you, head of G-2?"

Mbwato looked surprised. "Yes, as a matter of fact, I am. However could you tell?"

I sighed and swung the Ford over into the far right lane and headed up the curving exit that leads to Interstate 66. "I just guessed," I said.

"Mr. Ulado is my second in command. It's Captain Ulado really."

"The getaway expert," I said. "I hope he's better at that than he is at torture."

"Oh, he is," Mbwato said quickly, as if I'd just lodged a complaint that could turn into a hanging offense or, at least, a general court-martial. "He's really quite efficient."

We didn't say much after that as we rolled through northern Virginia, through the heart of the hunt country. Highway 29 and 211 was just another road, sometimes two lanes, sometimes four lanes, and lined by the usual Stuckey candy stands, billboards, gas stations, motels, and quiet, closed-mouthed houses stuck off by themselves as if their owners didn't mind living by the side of the road, but to hell with that friend-to-man nonsense.

At a sign that read WARRENTON, 5 MILES, I turned right and Mbwato said, "This person whom we're to see. Does he have a name?"

"Yes."

"Can you reveal it?"

"Yes. Winfield Spencer."

"Ah, I see."

"Do you?"

"Well, not really. But Mr. Spencer, I believe, is chairman of the Coulter Museum's executive committee and I seem to recall that one of his firms was interested in securing drilling rights in Komporeen. Am I right?"

"You are."

"Fascinating. Mr. Spencer has the shield?"

"Yes."

"And he is simply going to hand it over to you?"

"Uh-huh."

"Really fascinating," Mbwato said. "Someday you will have to tell me the full story."

"Someday," I said. "I will."

The road that we turned left on was a narrow, winding strip of asphalt that dipped and twisted between parallel rows of split-rail fences. There were a few unpretentious farmhouses and then the split-rail fences ended and were replaced on the left-hand side of the road by an eight-foot chain-wire fence that was topped by three wicked-looking strands of barbed wire. Behind the fence were pasture land and woods. No crops grew and I assumed that the Federal government paid Spencer not to grow anything. The chain-wire fence went on for two miles—which is a lot of fence to anyone but the military. At the two-mile point there was a stone hut with a thick, shake-shingled roof whose age was belied by the gray butt of an air conditioner which stuck out of one window. The road ended in a turnaround circle for the benefit of the strayed motorist out for a Sunday drive or for those who came calling on Spencer without an invitation. I stopped the car before the gate and the two men in gray uniforms came out of the hut and walked slowly over to the Ford. One of them, about thirty-five with gray, suspicious eyes that squinted underneath the brim of hat that seemed to have been copied from the highway patrol, rested his right arm on the window sill of the car and looked at me for several seconds. His partner circled around to Mbwato's side, opened the rear door, looked inside, and then stared at Mbwato, who gave him a nice sample of the glory smile.

"Mr. St. Ives?" the guard on my side of the car said, his left arm still leaning casually on the Ford's window ledge, his right hand resting not so casually on the butt of a holstered revolver.

"Yes."

"May I see some identification, please?"

I got out my wallet and handed him the New York driver's license. He read it without moving his lips and then handed it back. "The other gentleman?" From the way he said it I could tell that Mbwato was a mile or two from being a gentleman in his estimation.

"He wants some identification," I said.

"To be sure," Mbwato said, reached into the inside breast pocket of his splendid deep blue, raw-silk jacket, and handed over what looked to be a passport. The guard opened it, read all about Mbwato, looked at the picture, compared it with the real thing, and then said, "How do you pronounce it?"

"Conception Mbwato," the good colonel said in his best Old Boy English.

"Just a minute," the guard said, and went back into the hut and picked up a telephone. The other guard continued to lean on the door on the right-hand side and stare at Mbwato. "You're a big 'un, for sure," he said conversationally, and Mbwato smiled at him again. The guard in the hut replaced the phone and came out. "Follow the road straight ahead," he said, as if by rote. "Do not turn off. Do not drive over twenty miles per hour. Do not stop. One mile from here you'll be met by a blue jeep. Follow the jeep to the main house."

"Thanks," I said.

He nodded and went back into a hut where I assumed that he pressed a button because the two iron gates parted. I drove through and followed another winding asphalt road through grassland and forest for a mile. I drove exactly twenty miles per hour. There were no buildings in sight.

"Mr. Spencer seems to put a high premium on security," Mbwato said.

"His art collection is worth God knows how many million dollars," I said. "I guess he doesn't want it trucked away in the middle of the night."

"How large is his farm?"

"Plantation," I said.

"Sorry."

"Four thousand acres, I think. That's about eleven square miles."

"My word."

The blue jeep was waiting for us with a sign on its back that read FOLLOW ME, just like the ones that some airports have. Its driver was another of Spencer's lean, rangy home guards and he kept the jeep at exactly twenty miles per hour as we wound through the meadows and the pines and the oaks and the birches. Three miles from where we picked up the jeep we topped a rise and caught our first glimpse of what one can do to make oneself comfortable if one is worth a billion dollars or so.

It was built on the side of a hill that ran down to an artificial lake that was large enough to land the pontoon-equipped six-passenger Beechcraft that was tied up alongside a concrete dock. The house or mansion or villa or chateau or whatever it was carefully tumbled down the side of the hill for a hundred yards or so. It was built primarily of gray fieldstone that had been cut into massive blocks at least ten feet long and two feet high. Thick chimneys stuck up from the black slate roof here and there and the windows were recessed a foot into the stone under wide eaves that thrust the roof line out in a pleasantly aggressive manner. It was a one-story structure built on at least a dozen levels that wandered down to the lake. A brilliant green lawn was saved from looking as if you could putt on it by what seemed to be casual plantings of shrubs and flowers, which probably crowned the life's work of some landscape genius.

Separated from the house by some fifty yards was a large, windowless one-story structure of what looked to be gray marble. It was built on a ledge that had been cut into the hill and I assumed that it contained Spencer's art collection.

The jeep with the FOLLOW ME sign took us up a

crushed-stone drive that circled in front of two massive green copper doors that were recessed into the gray stone. The jeep stopped and I pulled up behind it. The guard came back to the Ford and bent down to look at us. "No packages, briefcases, or luggage are allowed inside," he recited. "If you will step out of the car, please."

I stepped out and he said, "Hold your arms straight out from your body, please." I did and he ran expert hands over me. "Thank you," he said, then turned to Mbwato and gave him the same instructions and the same treatment. Mbwato left his large, black attaché case on the front seat.

The guard went up three steps to the door, pressed a button, and spoke into an intercommunication device. "Cleared at primary checkpoint," he said. "Henderson now returning to mile-point-one." The communications device squawked something and the green doors were opened by a wide-shouldered, narrow-hipped man, about thirty, with short-cropped brown hair and a face that would have been almost pretty but for a nose that someone had broken. "Mr. St. Ives," he said, looking at me, "and Mr. Mbwato, I believe." I nodded. "I'm Mr. Spencer's secretary. Will you follow me, please."

Mbwato and I followed him down a wide carpeted hall to a closed door. He knocked on the door and then opened it, stood to one side, and motioned us through. I went first; Mbwato followed. It was a good-sized room, well furnished and richly carpeted. Opposite the door was a glass wall that afforded a view of the lake. A massive carved desk was at the far right. Behind the desk was Spencer and behind Spencer, resting on the floor and leaning against the wall, as if nobody could think of a place to hang it, was the shield of Komporeen.

Mbwato gave a long sigh as we moved toward the desk. Spencer stood up, glanced at the shield, and then looked at me. "You haven't seen it before, have you, St. Ives?"

"No."

"But Mr. Mbwato—or rather, Colonel Mbwato, I should say—has."

"Often," Mbwato said.

"You said that you were bringing no one who was of the police, St. Ives," Spencer said, and toyed with a letter opener on his desk. It was the only thing on it. "You lied to me."

"I did?"

"Yes, you did. Colonel Conception Mbwato is very much of the police. The Komporeenean police."

"I thought you were in the army," I said to Mbwato.

The big man smiled gloriously and shrugged. "In a small country such as mine, Mr. St. Ives, it is sometimes difficult to separate the duties of the constabulary from those of the armed forces."

"They have a name for Colonel Mbwato in his country," Spencer said. "They call him 'The Rope.'"

"Do they?" I said to Mbwato.

"Only the enemies of my country, I assure you, Mr. St. Ives."

"And there have been at least two thousand of them in recent months," Spencer said. "They have dangled from the end of ropes."

"History demonstrates that each revolution produces a fair crop of both traitors and patriots," Mbwato said. "It was at one time my duty to deal with the traitors."

I moved over to the shield, squatted down, and looked at it. I was surprised that it was a dull, dark green. But most brass that is nine hundred or so years old probably is. In the center of the shield was a sunburst and from it emanated in widening concentric circles carefully cast figures who seemed busy running, harvesting, planting, making love, and killing each other with sharp-looking knives and spears. I thought they were extremely well done, as were some animals who were also getting killed. It may have told a story, but there didn't seem to be much plot.

I stood up and turned to Spencer. "Anything else?"

"You may have cost me a great deal of money, St. Ives."

"I haven't thought about it."

"You will," he said, tightening his mouth into what I suppose he hoped was a grim line.

"Mr. Spencer has a flair for the dramatic, doesn't he?" Mbwato said.

I shrugged. "You want me to help carry the thing or would you rather do it yourself?"

"I can manage," Mbwato said.

"You'll never get another assignment, St. Ives," Spencer said. "I'll see to it."

Mbwato moved over to the shield, ran a large hand over its edge, then leaned it from the wall and slipped his left arm through two brackets on its back. He picked it up easily, all sixty-eight pounds, and I thought that it was a perfect fit.

"Do you have any more threats?" I said to Spencer.

He was staring at the shield and once again there was that look that I had seen twice before, once on the face of a fat man in a cafeteria and once on the face of a cop on the take in a New York hotel. Greed. Spencer ran a thin, pointed tongue over his lips as if he could taste it.

"It'll never get to Africa," he said. "He'll sell it in London or Rotterdam. He's fooled you, St. Ives. He hasn't fooled me. He'll sell it."

"Would you sell it in Rotterdam or London?" I asked Mbwato.

"How much, Mr. Spencer?" Mbwato said softly. "How much do you think it would bring—in Rotterdam, say?"

"How much do you want?" Spencer said in a whisper, his thin tongue working at his lips again. Mbwato stared back at him, holding the shield chest high, his face for once impassive. "How much?" Spencer said again, hurling the words into the silence. "How much do you want?" This time it was a scream, one that keened out on the last word.

Mbwato looked at him without expression. Then he smiled, that gleaming, brighten-the-corner-where-you-are smile of his, and turned toward the door. I followed him through it and down the hall.

Halfway to the green copper doors that were held open by the man with the broken nose, Spencer called after us. It was more of a scream than a call. "How much, Mbwato? How much do you want?"

We didn't hesitate or stop. We went through the door and down the three steps and across the crushed rock to the car. Mbwato put the shield in the rear, leaning it against the back seat. I had the car started by the time he got in next to me. "By the way," he said, "what time is it?"

I didn't look at my watch. I put the car into drive and pressed down on the accelerator. The rear wheels churned up some of the crushed rock. "It's getaway time," I said.

24

I kept the Ford at twenty miles per hour on the way to the gate. We went past the blue jeep and its guard only glanced at us.

"Do you think he'll give up so easily?" Mbwato said.

"Spencer? I don't know."

"At the gate perhaps," he said.

"What about the gate?"

"They could try to stop us there."

"He could have stopped us in the house. He's got enough help around."

"No," Mbwato said. "Not in his home. It would be too complicated. I think the gate and if so, one must be prepared." He took a key from his pocket and fitted it to the lock of his large attaché case. He opened it and I glanced at its contents.

"What in the hell is that?"

"Part of the Virginia contingency plan," he said. "A submachine gun. A Carl Gustaf M45 to be exact, manufactured in Sweden." He busily snapped things together. "Fires a 9-millimeter parabellum round, six hundred a minute. Thirty-six in the magazine," he said, clicking one into the breech or whatever it was. I'm sure Mbwato knew.

With its U-shaped metal stock folded over its right side, the Carl Gustaf M45 had a wicked look about it. "Only weighs a little over nine pounds," Mbwato said, handling the weapon as though it were an extension of his right arm.

"You get caught with a submachine gun in this country and you get thirty years," I said.

"Really? I have one for you."

"I don't know anything about them," I said.

"Oh, it's not a submachine gun. It's an automatic. Here."

I had to take my right hand off the wheel to accept his present. It was a surprisingly light automatic. I glanced at it and saw the name Colt engraved on its slide.

"Quite a good piece," Mbwato said. "It's the Colt .45 Commander model with the alloy frame. Weighs just 26 ounces. Wonderful stopping power."

"I don't know quite how to thank you," I said, and put the automatic on the seat beside me.

"Just a precaution."

"Is it loaded?"

"Of course."

The two guards at the exit to the plantation must have seen us coming because the gate opened as we approached and the one who earlier had examined our identification was outside the stone hut waving us through. Mbwato smiled at him as we went past; the guard didn't smile back. I pressed the accelerator down and the Ford jumped up to sixty miles an hour, which was really too fast for that road.

"Okay," I said, "where to?"

"When you get to Highway 29 and 211 turn left. What time is it now?"

I looked at my watch. "Eight-twenty."

"It's growing dark."

"Does that fit in with your getaway plan?"

"Perfectly," he said.

"That's good, because we're going to need it."

"Why?"

"We've got two cars behind us."

"They're following?"

"That's right."

"My word. Can you lose them?"

"No," I said. "I'd only lose myself."

Mbwato turned around in the seat. "There seem to be two in each car and they're wearing hats very much like the guards at Spencer's. He must have changed his mind."

"He must have."

"Is this a fast car?"

"Fairly so."

"Then I think we should go as fast as possible."

"That's what I'm doing. It might help if you told me where we're going."

"Bull Run," Mbwato said, adding dreamily, "'Look! There stands Jackson like a stone wall. Rally behind the Virginians.' General Barnard Elliott Bee said that, you know; gave Jackson his nickname."

"At Bull Run," I said.

"Manassas really. The first battle of Manassas to be exact. Jackson was an extremely dour man, most reserved."

"And that's where we're going? To Manassas?"

"Not to the town, to the battlefield."

"It was a big battle," I said. "What particular spot do you have in mind?"

"Henry Hill."

"What's on Henry Hill?"

"It's where Jackson held. In point of fact, there's a statue of him there now. Might have been the turn of the battle really. McDowell's union troops were hopeless, raw recruits mostly. Had McDowell kept the plateau, he might have won. There's been some debate about that. But it was a great victory for the South. Their first. In fact, it was the first battle of the war."

"It's not that I don't like your lecture, Colonel, but just what are we going to do when we get to Henry Hill? You know, where Jackson was first called Stonewall."

Mbwato turned in his seat to look out the rear window. "They seem to be gaining, don't they?"

"I was watching during your lecture."

"At Henry Hill we rendezvous with Captain Ulado."

"I take it you chose the spot."

"Yes. It's only about twelve air miles from Dulles International."

"How far by road?"

"We don't have to worry about that, Mr. St. Ives. Captain Ulado is meeting us with a helicopter."

I nodded, keeping my surprise to myself, and glanced in the rear-view mirror. The two cars behind us were maintaining their distance. The closer one was approximately a hundred feet behind the Ford. At the junction of Highway 29 and 211 I barely paused and then skidded the car into a left turn. I pressed the gas pedal down hard and when I next looked at the speedometer the needle was bounding off ninety-five.

"This is as fast as it'll go," I shouted at Mbwato above the engine and wind noise. He nodded, half turned in the front seat, the muzzle of the submachine gun resting on the seat's back.

Traffic was light and it got even lighter when most of the cars and trucks veered off to the right to take Interstate 66 rather than the slower 29 and 211. The two pursuing cars remained leeched to our rear, neither closer nor farther away. A mile past the cutoff to 66 they made their move. The lead car, a black monster that I thought to be an Oldsmobile, drew up effortlessly alongside us. The second car, another Oldsmobile, took up a position ten feet to the rear of the Ford's bumper. I was boxed. The car on the left swerved toward me and I had to hit the shoulder to avoid a sideswipe. I got the Ford back on the road. I didn't have the speed to move ahead. I couldn't slam on the brakes, so I decided to go after the car on the left, but he dropped back too quickly for me to make any move.

"Don't try it again," Mbwato yelled. "Just wait for him to draw alongside."

He clambered over the seat into the rear, taking the submachine gun with him. The lead Oldsmobile pulled up alongside me again and the machine gun went off in my ear.

"What the hell are you doing?" I screamed.

"Shooting at him. I believe I got the bugger."

I looked in my rear-view mirror. Both cars had dropped back, but not much. The man next to the driver in the lead car was talking over a telephone, probably to the car back of him about how they could head us off at the pass.

"You didn't hit anything," I yelled at Mbwato.

"What time is it?" he screamed in my ear. He had to scream because the submachine gun had made both my ears ring. I looked at my watch. "Eight-forty."

"Can't you go any faster?"

"No. How far?" I yelled.

"Five minutes."

I concentrated on my driving. Mbwato crawled back into the front seat and produced his map, which he studied by the light of the open glove compartment. It was growing dark, not quite dusk yet. I decided that the attempt to wreck us made sense. At least to Spencer. When a car goes out of control at ninety-five, few of its passengers walk away. We could be accidentally killed, his guards could retrieve the shield, even if it were somewhat damaged, and Spencer could go drilling for oil in Komporeen. A car wreck would be simple and safer than a bullet in his well-appointed house. No messy bodies to dispose of.

No one to wonder what happened to that itinerant go-between and the spade colonel with the funny name. They just died in a car wreck.

"That stone house ahead," Mbwato yelled. "Take a right."

I took a right, barely missing a stone pillar as the car slewed on its mushy springs. An asphalt road led up a hill. "Now where?"

Mbwato studied his map. "Next left; take the next left," he said.

I took the next left onto an even smaller road, the tires shuddering and squealing in protest. I glanced in the rear-view mirror. There was now only one car following.

The road ended abruptly near a white frame house. "Wrong road," Mbwato muttered. "Wrong goddamned road. Not your fault though. Mine. Never could read a map."

The black Oldsmobile had stopped fifty feet behind us, its two occupants wary of Mbwato's submachine gun. "What do we do now?" I said. "Make St. Ives' last stand?"

"Run for it," Mbwato said, jerking his door open.

"Where?"

"Up there," he said, pointing to a hill where I could see the outline of a statue of a man on a horse. "Henry Hill."

It was three hundred yards away, all uphill. Mbwato opened the rear door and snatched out the shield. He slipped it over his left forearm and waved the submachine gun at me. "Make a run for it."

There was a shot and the sound indicated that it came from near the parked Oldsmobile. The Ford's rear window cobwebbed around a hole. I snatched up the automatic from the seat and ran around the car. Mbwato stood at the edge of the road and fired two bursts at the Oldsmobile. There was an answering shot. And then another.

"Let's go," he said, and started running up gently

sloping Henry Hill, which boasted not a rock, not a tree, not a bush. I ran after him. I had no place else to go. We were a third of the way up the hill when I heard the helicopter. It came in low, barely skirted a forest of trees to the left and settled gently to the ground near the statue of what I assumed to be a horse and General Thomas Jonathan Jackson, who once had stood like a stone wall and later was carried across a river and into some trees to die at thirty-nine.

There were two more shots. They came from behind us. Mbwato stopped and turned. He held the sixty-eight-pound shield out at his left side and fired the machine gun from his right hip. A long burst. Then a short one. I turned to see a man in a gray uniform fall to his knees and then sprawl forward on the grass. The second man in a gray uniform flopped to his belly. He carried a rifle and he seemed to be taking careful aim from the prone position. He fired once; then twice. Mbwato's machine gun let off a burst and I turned. He stood there for a moment, a big, black man in a blue silk jacket, an African brass shield on one arm, a Swedish submachine gun cradled in the other. He stood there and lifted his face up to the sky and roared a long terrible cry. Then he fell backward onto the grass that sloped gently up to the top of Henry Hill where the helicopter and Stonewall Jackson waited for the black colonel who had a sneaking sympathy for the Confederacy.

I turned to face the man with the rifle. He was up on one knee and I lifted the automatic and squeezed the trigger twice, then three times, then four. It was luck. You shouldn't hit anything at that distance with an automatic, but the third or the fourth bullet caught him and he dropped the rifle and clutched his stomach and then bent slowly forward to the ground.

I ran to Mbwato who lay face up on the grass. There were two small red stains, about the size of dimes, on his white shirt, just to the right of its buttons. He breathed harshly and his breath bubbled in his throat.

"Take it," he said.

"Take what?" I said.

"The shield, you fool."

"How bad?" I said. "How bad is it?"

"The shield, damn it," he said, and lifted it up, all sixty-eight pounds of it, with his left arm. I tugged it off and put it on the grass.

"Take it to Ulado," he said. "He'll know what to do."

"Okay," I said.

He looked at me with those curiously gentle dark eyes, the man they called "The Rope," and then he smiled that come-to-glory smile. "You have been, Mr. St. Ives, most gracious," he said, and then he died.

I knelt there in the grass beside him just staring, and then there was a shout from the helicopter. I stuffed the automatic into my coat pocket, picked up the shield with both hands, and started toward the helicopter. I couldn't see anything. The shield was in front of my eyes. I heard a shot. And then there was another and something twanged off the shield, knocking me backward. I dropped the shield. Two men in gray were coming down the hill from the right. Both held rifles and both of them were aimed at me. I pulled the automatic out of my pocket and fired blindly, but the two men continued to advance slowly, one careful pace at a time. They were still fifty feet away when I threw the automatic at them and bent down for the shield. As I straightened, one of them put his rifle to his shoulder and took careful aim. There was a sudden burst of fire from the helicopter and both of the gray-clad men dropped to the grass. I couldn't tell whether they were hit. I didn't care. I ran toward the helicopter. It wasn't much of a run, not carrying sixty-eight pounds of brass uphill. A child could have caught me, a toddler. It was almost dark now and I guided myself by the sound of the helicopter and the light in its plastic-domed nose.

Hands reached out and took the shield from me.

"Inside, Mr. St. Ives," a voice said, and I recognized it as belonging to Mr. Ulado, who lifted the shield into the rear of the four-place machine. When it was stowed away he picked up a submachine gun that was the twin of the one that Mbwato had had and in a casual, practiced way loosed another burst at the two men with rifles.

"They must have circled around," I said, because I couldn't think of anything else to say.

"Get in," Ulado said. "Where's Mr. Mbwato?"

"He's dead," I said. "Halfway up Henry Hill."

"You're sure?"

"Yes."

"Get in."

I climbed into the back. Ulado got in the seat next to the pilot, a slim young Negro who wore a green velour shirt and a coconut straw hat with a plain black band. "Dulles," Ulado barked at him, and the young Negro nodded and shot the helicopter up.

Ulado turned around in his seat to face me. "The pilot," he yelled. "Trained in Vietnam." I nodded and sank back in the hard canvas seat. It was a short hop, not more than ten minutes, if that. The pilot talked over his radio to the tower and set the copter down not far from the main terminal. Ulado got out and I crawled after him. He reached into the cockpit of the machine and wrestled the shield out.

"Mbwato said you'd know what to do with it," I said.

Captain Ulado nodded gravely. "I do, Mr. St. Ives. May I thank you for all your help. We say good-by here. I have a plane standing by on the runway." He put the shield down so that it rested against his left leg and held out his right hand. I shook it.

"You'll never know how much we appreciate your efforts," he said, picked up the shield, turned, and walked off into the dark. I started to call after him, to tell him that he'd forgotten his submachine gun, but perhaps he didn't need it any more.

I walked toward the terminal, found my way up to the main lobby, and then located someone who could tell me what I wanted to know. "You have a chartered plane leaving here in a few minutes with a friend of mine on board," I said. "I think it's a prop job."

The man in blue uniform flipped through some cards on the counter. "Yes," he said. "A Constellation. Chartered by a Mr. Mbwato—I think that's how you pronounce it." He turned and looked at the wall behind him. "It should be departing any moment now."

"Could you tell me its destination?" I said.

"Sure," he said. "Rotterdam."

25

At eight o'clock the next morning I was lying in a bed in the room at the Madison, staring up at the ceiling, and waiting for someone to come and take me away when the telephone rang. It was a Miss Schulte, who said that she worked for Hertz.

"The car that you reported stolen has been found in Silver Spring, Mr. St. Ives. That's in Maryland. It was undamaged except for the rear window, which apparently has a bullet hole in it."

"I wonder how that got there?" I said.

She said that she didn't know but that the insurance would take care of it. Then she asked whether I would like to come down to pay for the rental or would I like her to bill me. I told her to bill me and she said that would be fine.

"And the next time you need a car, Mr. St. Ives, be sure to call Hertz." I promised that I would and hung up.

I hadn't reported the car as being either missing or

stolen so I assumed that Spencer's gray-clad private troopers had tidied things up when they got through shooting at me. I also assumed that they had collected the bodies, picked up the spent shell cases, and even policed the area for old cigarette butts before driving the rented Ford to Silver Spring and dumping it there. I wondered what they had done with Mbwato and whether anyone would ever come looking for him, but a billion dollars could hide almost anything, even a dead body as large as that of the colonel from Komporeen who, when alive, may have been the world's most accomplished liar. I spent a few moments speculating about how much the Dutch-British combine would pay Captain Ulado for the shield in Rotterdam and whether he would spend some of it in Corfu or Acapulco, and if, while spending it, he would ever think about the children with distended bellies who went around eating mud, straw, twigs, and chalk. I felt that if he did think about it, it wouldn't bother him much, no more than it would have bothered Colonel Mbwato.

I called down for some breakfast and *The Washington Post* and when they came I read a brief story about how the caretaker at the Manassas National Battlefield Park last night had reported hearing a series of gunshots near the statue of Stonewall Jackson, but after investigating, police said that they had found nothing. I was pouring my third cup of coffee when someone knocked at the door. It was Lieutenant Demeter wearing a green sport shirt and light gray slacks.

"My day off," he said as he came in the room, looked around with his cop's eyes, and selected a comfortable chair.

"Coffee?" I said.

"Sure. Black."

I handed him a cup and then went back to my chair. "Haven't found it yet," Demeter said, and sipped at his coffee.

"What?"

"The shield."

"Oh."

"You don't seem much interested, St. Ives."

"I'm not any more. The Coulter Museum has decided that it no longer needs my services, such as they are."

Demeter nodded and placed his cup and saucer on a table. "That's what the Wingo woman told me last night. I gave her a call because I was trying to find you. She was kind of shook up, said that you gave her a rough time—almost accused her of being in on the whole thing."

"Just talk," I said.

"That all?"

"That's all."

"Uh-huh," Demeter said. "That's what I figured. Reason I was calling you yesterday, I wanted to tell you about your two little pals."

"What pals?"

"The kid and his girl. The thieves."

"What about them?"

"They got a lawyer."

"So?"

"Well, he's not a lawyer, he's about the best that money can buy. A whole lot of money."

"Who?"

"Wilfred Coley."

"That's a whole lot of money," I said.

"So I was wondering who was going to pick up his tab."

"Ask Coley," I said.

"He won't say."

"You're asking me?"

"That's right, St. Ives, I'm asking you."

"I don't know," I lied. It would be Spencer, of course, still tidying things up.

"I think you do," Demeter said.

"I'm out of it, Lieutenant, all the way out."

Demeter leaned back in his chair and clasped his hands behind his head. He looked relaxed, rested, and unhurried. It was his day off and he had no place better to go. "It should be real interesting," he said.

"What?"

"Watching Coley work on you."

"Me?"

"At the trial. You'll be a key witness for the prosecution."

"I hadn't thought about it."

"He'll cut you up into little pieces. Little, bitty ones."

"He's good, I understand."

"He'll turn you inside out and every way but loose. But, of course, you're smart. You won't tell him anything but the truth. Just like you're telling me. Oh, you might leave out a little—like the two spades and their curling iron. You might leave that out."

"It never happened," I said.

"Course not. So you might as well leave it out. And then you might leave out about the shield."

"What about it?"

"That you know where it is."

"I don't know where it is."

"The Wingo woman said that you told her and Spencer that you knew where it was, but that you'd tell only Spencer. Did you?"

"Ask him," I said. "I don't know where it is."

Demeter unclasped his hands from behind his head and waved his right one at me in what he must have hoped was a reassuring gesture. It wasn't. "Don't worry about me, St. Ives. By the time this thing goes to trial, that shield will have been almost forgotten. It's murder now and nobody's going to be too worried about what happened to a brass shield. Nobody but me anyhow. But I can't prove anything. I can make some guesses, some pretty good ones, I think, but they're still just guesses and I'm not even sure that I'd prove anything if I could. You know why?"

"Why?" I said.

"Because you didn't make anything out of it, did you?"

"No."

He nodded his head and smiled in a well-satisfied sort of way. "Nobody made anything, did they?"

"Not to my knowledge."

He smiled again and if the dog in the manger had a smile, it must have been very much like the one that Demeter wore. "That's what I thought. The hot-shot, big-time, New York City go-between. You had it all there, I bet, right in your hands and you didn't make a dime, did you? Not a dime."

"No," I said.

He nodded again, almost happy now. "Like I said," Demeter went on, "I think I got most of it figured out. You take the two spades with their limey accents and their curling iron, add somebody with enough money —and enough interest—to hire Coley to defend the kid and his girl, throw in the fact that the Wingo woman's husband had a hell of a big habit that he had to feed, and somehow it all hangs together. A little loose maybe, but together."

"I'm glad," I said.

"I bet. There're still a couple of pieces missing, of course. But it's not bad, not bad at all. You want to know what my picture looks like?"

"No," I said. "Not much. Not at all, in fact."

He nodded thoughtfully, picked up his cup of coffee, drained it, put it back down, and rose. He moved easily, I noticed, as though he had had a good night's sleep. He probably didn't even dream. "Just a couple of more questions, St. Ives. Just a few more off the record, like they say. Only you and me now. Nobody else. Like I said, I can't prove anything and I'm not sure I want to prove anything, not if I might have to go up against a billion dollars."

"What questions?" I said.

"What you did there at the end for nothing, it didn't

230

turn out the way you thought it would, did it?"

"No."

He moved slowly to the door, his head bent forward as if deep in thought. Then he turned and stared at me once more with his beany black eyes. "But you could have made a buck or two. I mean it was lying around and you could have skimmed some off?"

"Yes," I said. "I suppose so."

He paused at the door as if deciding how to phrase the next question and when he said it, he said it slowly and carefully as if counting each word. "Then if it wasn't for money, why did you go ahead and do it, I mean, a guy like you?"

I looked at him for a while before answering. He seemed to be in no hurry. "Cotton candy and hungry kids, perhaps," I said. "Or sick kittens and lost puppies."

Demeter nodded slightly, as if he thought that he might understand, but wasn't really sure. "Well, I guess that's an answer," he said. "As much of one as I should expect."

"That's all it is," I said. "Just an answer."

I never did think up a better one, not even after Demeter left and I stood there for a long time with my hand on the phone trying to decide whom I should call in Rotterdam. Or whether I should call anyone at all.